Acknowledgment

I'd like to thank my fans for allowing me the opportunity to do what I love. I want to thank my family for being there for me. I appreciate your sacrifice in my journey as well. I want to thank God for blessing me with a gift and desire to write. Enjoy!

Last Goodbye

Raheim

I stood at the window watching my aunt Sadie and my girl Felicia step into the black limo parked in front of the house. Today was my baby brother's funeral and I didn't feel like going. With one last look in the mirror I walked through my aunt's house like a zombie. I ignored all of the well-wishers and offers of condolences from my aunt's neighbors as I stepped into the back of the limo. All eyes were on me as I sat beside Felicia. She looked good in her black knee length dress and swollen belly. It's crazy how life plays out. In the same moment I lost my brother I found out I would be a dad with the only woman I cared about in this world.

My aunt Sadie reached over and squeezed my hand. I couldn't feel anything, a week before I had to rescue my brother from a crazy bitch looking to pay me back for kicking her dude's ass. Now I was driving in the front of a

Platinum

Dust 2

By: K.C. Blaze

Platinum Dust 2

-A Novel Written by-
K.C. Blaze

Copyright © 2015 K.C. Blaze
Published by K.C. Blaze Publishing

platinumfiction@yahoo.com
Twitter: @26kcblaze

This novel is a work of fiction. Any resemblances to actual events, real people, living or dead, organizations, establishments or locales are products of the author's imagination. Other names, characters, places, and incidents are used fictitiously.

Cover Design: AMB Branding
Editor: Sharon Wethington Sargent

Because of the dynamic nature of the Internet, any Web addresses or links contained in this book may have changed since publication, and may no longer be valid. The views expressed in this work are solely those of the author and do not necessarily reflect the views of the publisher and the publisher hereby disclaims any responsibility for them.

funeral procession. I fought back the memory of my brother choking on his own blood in the back of a getaway car as we headed toward the church holding his body. As the limo made its way to the church I noticed how crowded the streets were. There were lots of faces I didn't recognize. Amir was well known at his church and many of its members came out to wish him farewell. I made sure his funeral was one of a kind. He had a white casket with gold plated letters spelling out his name on the side. We would even release doves when the pall bearers carried his casket to the hearse. When the limo parked in front of the church we stepped out and I forced my legs to push me forward. Family would get a private viewing and then they would allow others to come in.

My girl Felicia stood beside me the entire time holding my hand. When I stopped walking she stopped also. She knew how hard this was for me. Amir was my only brother from a mother I hated for killing my father and kicking me out of the house at eleven and a father who was dead way before his time. My aunt walked into the front of the church toward the casket and I could hear her crying loudly. I choked back the lump growing in my throat as I waited for her to come back out. Moments later she walked out with mascara lines running down her face. I knew this was hard for my aunt, first losing my dad her- only brother, then her husband a few years ago, and now, my brother that she raised like a son.

When I was finally able to muster up enough courage to go in the large room I inched forward with slow deliberate steps. Felicia hung back to close the doors to give me privacy.

I walked up to the casket closing my eyes for a moment. I couldn't believe how peaceful he looked. His hair was freshly cut and his all white suit looked good on him. I had to admit he was a pretty good looking kid. His last words 'Are you lying about seeing Janet?' rushed into my mind like a rushing river knocking me to my knees. He was happy knowing that I went to visit our mom Janet after all of the years of trying to reunite us.

I cried uncontrollably at the feet of my brother's casket. Felicia stood beside me stroking my hair.

God I asked you to let him be ok! I couldn't believe this shit. How could he be dead? I could only be mad at myself. The doors opened but I didn't look up until I felt Felicia's grip on my shoulder tighten.

Janet Starz escorted by two correctional officers walked in wearing a black two piece dress suit in true dramatic form. She walked to the casket like she couldn't believe what she was seeing. She lye across Amir's body weeping like she was the only one there. For a moment I felt sorry for the lady I grew to hate over the last 15 years. After her crying spell she stood up and wiped Amir's suit.

"Raheim, how you holding up?" she asked and I wanted to ignore her question but I could feel Felicia watching me. I stood up off the floor and did what my brother would have wanted and wrapped my arms around the same woman who threw me out into the streets. I only let her cry into my shoulder for a few moments before I pushed her back and said.

"Sorry for the loss of your only son." I could feel the venom pulsing through her blood as she stared at me with hatred. Janet Starz was only an egg donor and my brother's death wouldn't change that. I reached for my girl's hand and turned to leave the viewing room.

"Let's go find my mom."

Fuck Being Nice

Janet

It was my mom who gave me the news about Amir and my heart shattered into a million pieces. Seeing him lying lifeless but still handsome in the white casket devastated me. The small amount of comfort Raheim offered with his hug was short lived as he made his hatred known. If the guards weren't standing so close by I would have lashed out at him for disrespecting me.

It was like being rejected by Carlos all over again. Every time I saw Raheim he managed to make me feel the same way his father did. The buff correctional officer gave me a few moments to say my final goodbyes to my baby boy before escorting me back to the prison bus. I wasn't allowed to stay for the service and that broke me up inside. It was time to get out and if I didn't have Raheim's help I would do it the old fashioned way, snitching!

I knew enough about a few big time hustlers to make a deal. With a tear streaked face I walked by a large crowd all coming to say goodbye to my baby and it caused me to lose my composure. I imagined it being Carlos' funeral and being able to ride in the limo like only his wife could.

My time was served and if no one else cared about me being locked up I would take care of myself. The long ride back to the cold building I've been calling home for the last fifteen years was getting closer and closer. Seeing all of the streets I grew up on brought a wave of homesickness I couldn't explain. I bit the inside of my jaw to stop myself from crying. I felt like a ghost of the past that no one could see but all but forgot about.

After being searched and processed I was escorted back to my cell where I walked over to my cot and laid down. I didn't want to be bothered and everyone there respected that. Though I felt lost without the only man who still thought I was worthy of forgiveness I would honor him by walking the streets of the free world again. His death wouldn't be in vain especially since he worked so hard to reconnect me and Raheim. Grateful, the other chicks there gave me my space. I used the time to reflect on my situation and how Raheim treated me. He was more like his father than I remember. Knowing that it was so easy for him to turn his back on me didn't sit easy. Carlos also thought it was that easy and we all knew how that ended. *Fuck being nice!* I shouted in my head.

Tough Questions

Felicia

During the service a pretty brown skinned girl cried uncontrollably at the back of the church. Her cries were almost loud enough to drown out the pastor. It was nice to hear the minister share all of the good things Amir did in his short life. I watched as Raheim sat stone faced beside me. I knew he was trying to hold it together but I would be there when he was ready to mourn. After the service we drove over to the cemetery. There were so many people in the funeral procession we needed a two police car escort.

As his casket was being lowered into the ground, well-wishers tossed single roses into the shallow grave. I squeezed his Aunt's hand to show my support. As we walked back toward the limo Dre pulled Rah off to the side. I stood waiting but couldn't hear what they were talking about. Raheim's face snapped in the direction of the chick who wouldn't stop crying and back to Dre. I wondered what that was about. I would have to ask later. For now I would wait for him to share what he was ready to share.

Raheim, his aunt and I piled into the back of the limo where Aunt Sadie reached over and grabbed him by the hand.

"His service was beautiful." She complimented softly.

"I think he would've liked it." Raheim stated with a lack of emotion, which scared me.

"Driver, take my aunt back to her house." Rah ordered the limo driver. We were all silent as we made our way back over to her house. When we pulled up the driver got out to open the door for her, she turned to face us.

"Aren't you coming in for something to eat?" she asked rhetorically.

"I can't be around all these people right now." He answered honestly.

"I understand. I'll call you later." She said before walking toward her house and the growing group of people arriving at her place.

The moment the driver closed the car door Raheim started speaking angrily.

"Did you see Janet's ass? She acted like she expected me to be there for her like she was around all these years. That bitch must have lost her fucking mind." He ranted.

"Well now you don't have to worry about her anymore." I said as he laid his head on my chest. I wondered if he realized he was stroking my belly.

Since everything that happened with Amir we haven't talked about the pregnancy. I was still not sure who told him but I was sure the conversation would come up some time soon.

"Take me home." He spoke to the driver.

"All I know is that her ass better not try to reach out to me again." He continued his rant. It was clear that he planned on not having anything else to do with her. The glue that held Janet and Raheim together was just buried and there was no going back. I wouldn't be the one to force him to be involved with the woman who threw him away so easily. I didn't know his mother's story, only want he told me but I knew that every woman who gets pregnant isn't meant to be a mother. We arrived at Rah's apartment complex in twenty minutes and I couldn't help but remember the last time I was here. The last time I walked out of this building I was telling him goodbye while holding the bloody clothes that got us into this mess. This time I was walking in as his woman. We walked the stairs to his apartment and I waited for him to open the door.

"You good?" he asked as I looked around the faintly familiar room.

"Can I have a glass of water?" I asked. He walked toward the kitchen as I sat on his plush couch.

When he came back into the room he sat beside me and pulled me into him as he passed me the bottled water.

"Thanks for being here for me." He spoke into my hair.

"I wouldn't be anywhere else."

"Can I ask you something babe?" he asked with a serious tone.

"Sure."

"Why didn't you tell me you were pregnant?" he asked casually. My heart caught in my throat.

Closing Doors

Raheim

I had no anger or animosity about Felicia not telling me she was pregnant but I did want to hear her answer. She pulled away from me and sat quiet for a brief moment.

"Look Rah, I didn't tell you because I knew how you felt about having a baby. I was ready to raise the kid on my own because I'm not about to force something on you that you weren't ready for." She explained. I smirked at her answer.

"I get it. I've done a lot of fucked up shit in this world but you're the only woman I would ever want to have my children. And despite how big your head is I'm in love with you." I joked to lighten the mood. She pushed my arm playfully before resting her head back on my chest.

"Your damn head is big, I didn't want to say anything but I'm worried about the baby looking like you." She said making us both laugh. I swear I love this girl. She was the only person I felt safe around and her being here for me right now made me love her more.

"Do you think we should be there with your aunt right now?" She changed the subject.

"I don't want to be around a bunch of people telling me how good my brother is or was right about now. It's my fault he's gone and I have to live with that shit for the rest of my life." I said. My voice cracked and my eyes began to water but I resisted the urge to cry. I had to figure out a way to move beyond this or I'd go crazy. My cell started to ring. I took a quick look at my phone to see Kelly's name flash across the screen. I hit the end button but she called right back.

"Give me a minute." I stood up and walked to the kitchen.

"Hello?" I answered.

"About damn time. Why you been avoiding me Raheim?" she asked, voice full of frustration.

"I already told your ass I'm done so technically it's not avoiding. Why the fuck you keep calling me Kelly?" I snapped.

"I told you I'm not letting your ass go that easy. I love you boo, so stop playing." She cooed into the phone.

"I ain't got time for this shit, my brother just died and I'm not doing this with you right now. Stop calling me."

"Oh my God! Baby I'm sorry. I didn't know about your brother honey. If you come over I can make you feel better." She ignored the part about not calling again. I was convinced her ass really was crazy. Without responding I ended the call.

"Remind me to change my number okay?" I told Felicia as I walked back into the living room. She was laying back on the couch. Now that I knew she was pregnant her belly looked more round, her skin looked more flawless and I wanted to protect her and my baby from anything and everything that could potentially be dangerous.

"C'mon let's go into the room, you can lay down in there or prop your feet up. You hungry?" I said as I began to unbutton my dress shirt.

"Yes, but I have a taste for some Wheaties and a fruit cup." She said it with excitement in her voice.

"Wheaties? I don't have no damn Wheaties." I said with a smirk on my face.

"But that's what I want." She pouted. To be honest I enjoyed having her here with me and if Wheaties is what she wanted then that's what she was going to get.

"Alright let me change and I'll take a ride to the store real quick." I promised.

When we reached my bedroom I went through one of the drawers and pulled out one of my larger t-shirts and passed it to her.

"You can wear this tonight." She took the shirt and swept her hair to one side of her shoulder before asking if I could unzip her black dress. I walked up behind her, taking my time I slowly unzipped her dress. My hands eased the straps of her dress down over her shoulders. I took a moment to hold her with both hands touching her stomach. This shit is starting to get real.

"We need to make a doctor's appointment." She rested her head on my chest as we stood in front of my bed.

"You coming?" she asked.

"Of course." I promised. Both my parents entered my mind when I thought of myself being a dad. *Fuck them!* I said to myself.

"Let me hurry up back with your box of Wheaties. Anything else before I leave." I kissed her on the cheek. She turned around to face me with a sexy ass smile playing on her lips.

"I think that's it for now. Just hurry up back." She pulled her dress down until it fell to the floor. I stood there staring at her beautiful dark skin, swollen belly and felt amazed that she was mine.

I turned to leave to head to the store while she changed clothes. The moment I sat in my car, thoughts of the conversation I had with Dre filled my thoughts. When he pulled me off to the side he let me know that he recognized the girl crying uncontrollably. He wasn't 100% sure yet but he believed she was there that night in the warehouse.

I told him to find out, because if she was I wanted her handled. There was no way she was going to walk the earth when my brother couldn't. I sped off in the direction of the store to get my baby what she wanted. Though I was mad as hell about my brother I was surprisingly happy about being a father. Seeing Felicia drink all of those virgin beverages in Jamaica should have been a tipoff.

The store was empty as I walked through looking for cereal. I spotted Beverly walking through the cereal aisle. There wasn't much I had to say to her, though I was grateful she told me about Felicia and the baby.

"Hey Raheim." She greeted first.

"Hey, what's up?" I asked rhetorically.

"Nothing much, is everything ok with you and Felicia? I haven't heard from her in a few days." She questioned.

"She's good, I'll tell her to hit you up." I stated before moving on to find a box of Wheaties.

Twenty minutes later and I was walking back into my apartment.

"I'm back, you up?" I shouted when I didn't see her on the couch. She walked into the living room in my t-shirt making me smile.

"Yeah, I'm up." Her face lit up when she saw the box of Wheaties.

"I saw your girl Beverly at the store." I said, walking to get her a bowl and spoon from the kitchen.

"She said you ain't been calling her so I told her you would." I informed her.

"Yeah, I'll give her a call later today." She sat down to eat.

"I can't believe it's only been a few days since she told me you were pregnant and I lost Amir." I said, amazed at how fast time flies.

"She did what?" Felicia snapped to attention.

"What? She told me you were pregnant when I was in the hospital." I said confused. What is the big deal?

"Are you serious?" she asked clearly mad.

"Why you worrying about it babe? I ain't mad." I tried to calm her down but she was already pissed.

Until Death Do Us Part

Felicia

Though my craving for Wheaties was strong, the desire to slap the hell out of Beverly was stronger. I couldn't believe what Rah just told me. I've been fighting forever to tell him that I was pregnant and she just goes in and share my business without checking with me first. With all the nonsense going on around Amir's death I still didn't feel like I could breathe yet. There was no question about me checking Beverly for the slip of her tongue but I guess I should be grateful.

He didn't have to tell me who was on the phone earlier and I didn't need to ask because I already knew it was a chick he was seeing. We would have that conversation at a later time but for now I was going to sit down to my cereal and enjoy his company.

"I'm going to make another doctor's appointment, it's about that time" I said in his direction.

"What do you think we're having?" he asked curiously, reaching for the box of Wheaties to pour himself a bowl.

"I don't know but I hope it's a girl." I said wishfully.

"Well if Amir was right and there is a God I think he'd know that I need a son." he said, happy with the thought of another him running around.

It was hard to believe that just a week and a half ago I was in Jamaica soaking up the sun, good food and Raheim's company. Knowing why we were really home was too difficult to think about so I shook the feeling. After we ate our cereal I washed the bowls and spoons while Rah stripped down to his boxers and socks before sitting on the sofa and holding out his arms to me. He wrapped his arms around my shoulders.

"Are you sure about this Raheim?" I asked looking him dead in the eye. With all sincerity he returned my gaze.

"Felicia, I couldn't be more sure about you, the baby and us. My brother would have loved." His voice cracked for the first time since this morning at the viewing. I laid my head on his chest.

"Shhhhh, its okay babe. I'm gonna love you past your pain and we're going to start our own family." I tried to comfort him. Rah was good at hiding his pain but he never held back from me. All I want to do is love him, it was in this moment that I promised myself that I would love him until death do us part.

It's A Small World

Raheim

It's been a full two weeks since Amir's funeral and me and Felicia have been living together in my apartment. We've been going back and forth from her place and mine. Though I used to run from a committed relationship it was growing on me. My Aunt Sadie welcomed Felicia into the family with open arms which made me more comfortable.

We were on our way to our first doctor's appointment together. The good thing about having the baby was the distraction it caused. I didn't tell Felicia that I had nightmares about Amir choking on his own blood in the backseat of that car. I didn't tell her that his face haunted me.

"Do you think we should wait to hear the sex of the baby?" Felicia asked.

"Hell no, I'm not waiting for another two and a half months to know if it's a boy or girl." I reached over and squeezed her hand. Pregnancy looked good on her.

"Fine but once you know what it is you have to promise to start working on a nursery." She said with a sexy ass smile spread across her face. I agreed as I pulled into a parking space by the entrance.

We gave our names to the brown haired nurse sitting behind the receptionist desk. She handed us a clipboard to fill out. Now that Felicia no longer worked at her job because no woman of mine was going to have to work unless she wanted to. Losing my brother changed me. I no longer felt like being with multiple women was the right thing to do and more importantly especially knowing that Felicia was seriously the only woman I cared enough about to be with.

We both filled out the long ass form that really only cared about her having medical insurance. None of that mattered because I was paying cash. We had to sit for another twenty minutes after handing over the clipboard before her name was called.

"Please have a seat." Dr. Demonte said while pointing toward the hospital bed. Something about being here made me feel caged and it didn't help that the doctor looked familiar. The room made me uncomfortable. Though my injury was only a flesh wound it still ached as a reminder of what I just went through.

"How are you feeling?" He asked Felicia.

"I'm good, I've been craving ice chips a lot though." She answered. Her round belly more noticeable.

"That's pretty normal. Your cravings are a bit more normal compared to some of the more extreme cases I've seen. I've noticed that you haven't been in to see us for a few months." He said while looking down at his clipboard.

"We were in Jamaica for a few weeks." I spoke up for her. The doctor looked my way for the first time.

"Beautiful place. Whelp, I'm gonna step out for you to change into this hospital gown and we can get your ultrasound done right away." The uneasy look on his face made me zoom in on his features, then it hit me that he was an old client of mine. He knew what I did for a living and I knew what he liked behind closed doors. I was tempted to lift Felicia off the bed and say his perverted ass wasn't touching her but then I would have to explain why I knew him.

Though I shared almost everything with her she still didn't know exactly what I did for a living. I knew she would disagree and I seriously didn't want her looking at me differently. Thoughts of leaving the business altogether ran through my mind but I've never had a job so corporate America wasn't going to be my plan B. I have enough money stashed away to live pretty for a few years but you can never be too careful.

After she changed into the gown the doctor knocked twice on the wooden room door. He peaked his head in before walking in. I stood on the side of Felicia and watched as the doctor squeezed a big glob of clear ultrasound gel on her stomach. He placed the monitor on her belly and right away a heartbeat filled the room. My heart stopped for a moment and for a brief second there was no one else in the room but me and our child. Felicia reached up and grabbed my hand with a big smile on her face.

"That's the baby's head right there." The doctor pointed to the monitor.

"Yeah he has your big ole' head" Felicia joked making me smile.

"Would you like to know the sex?" the doctor turned to face Felicia who then turned to look at me.

"Yes, we would." I answered. He began moving his hand around until he was in a position to see clearer. Without a question we were having a boy.

"It looks like you're having a boy." He confirmed what I already knew. In that moment I vowed to be the best father any kid could have, which meant I would have to clean up my life.

After a few more minutes of looking over the monitor the doctor gave her a once over and sent us to the receptionist to schedule another visit for next month. I asked the nurse to give me an estimate for the visit's payment and she told me roughly seven hundred dollars. I pulled out my rubber band bank and counted seven, one hundred dollar bills.

"I want a receipt." I said knowing that if I walked out they could still try to send Felicia a bill. The nurse wrote me out a receipt and slid it across her desk. Her eyes were wide with noticeable interest. Once we left the office

Felicia couldn't stop smiling the entire way to the car. Her hands stroked her belly making me want her. The minute we were both seated in the car I leaned over and kissed her. She leaned forward and pulled me closer with her hand on the back of my neck.

"Let's go over to the mall to pick out something for the baby." I offered. She lit up, kissing me one last time.

Oh Hell No!

Kelly

Tired isn't the word. I'm tired of Raheim treating me like he doesn't know I exist. I've been his ride or die all of this time and now he wants to start fronting. Well if he thought I was leaving him that easy he would be sadly mistaken. Work has been keeping me super busy so I wasn't able to pursue him as badly as I wanted to. If I could just get him back to my house where I could lay the pussy on him all would be good again.

He needed a reminder of what was important to him. Besides I missed the dick and he knew it, I couldn't keep telling my girls about how in love he was without showing them proof. I strutted over to my car in the company parking lot and hit the unlock button from my keychain. I stepped out of my heels before getting into the car. I left a little earlier after faking a headache. It was Tuesday, me and Rah's special day and I wanted to get a jump on calling him.

His number was on speed dial so I hit the button and waited for an answer before pulling off. It went to voicemail after the fourth ring. I hated hearing his answering service. I dialed again prepared to curse him out on his machine if he didn't answer this time. It went to voicemail again.

"Raheim I'm gonna need you to stop ignoring me. I don't know why the fuck you fighting it. We're meant to be together." I hit the end button and drove out of the parking lot towards home. My phone rang and I answered without looking at the screen.

"Rah?"

"No girl, you all whipped and shit." My best friend Shay's voice came through the phone.

"Whatever, I was waiting for Rah to call me back. What's up?" I asked. I knew she would be calling when I sent her the text that I was leaving early.

"Nothing trick, was you still going to Lakeisha's white party? Cause you gone need to buy some new shoes after what happened to your other pair." She asked. *Damn!* I almost forgot about my girl's white party.

"Yeah, I'm going but I'ma have to stop to get a pair now then." I answered.

"Did you invite Raheim?" She asked with a hint of sarcasm.

"Not yet but I will. Let me go I'm driving." I ended the call before she started asking me too many damn questions.

Midway down the street I took a sharp right turn and headed in the direction of Franklin Mills Mall. I wanted to hit up a few stores to see if they were running any sales. There is nothing worse than paying full price for a pair of shoes. Thirty minutes later I found myself pulling into a parking space a few rows from the entrance. The urge to call Raheim one more time was overwhelming but I fought the feeling. Grabbing my heels from the passenger seat I slipped them on and stepped out of my car, grabbing my wallet on my way out.

"Hey mami." A male voice yelled out in my direction. I didn't even turn to give him any indication that he had a chance.

Putting a bit more sway in my hips I strutted over toward the entrance. Something caught my attention the closer I got to the door. The image of Raheim walking down the stairs with a noticeably pregnant dark skinned chick on his arm. My feet froze first before my brain registered what I was seeing. He was smiling and my heart melted before I followed his gaze and noticed that it was her he was smiling at.

Without thinking I charged in their direction.

"Oh fucking really Raheim? You out here with this bitch and I've been calling your ass. Are you fucking kidding me?" I screamed catching him off guard. Both eyes were now on me and Raheim looked at me with eyes full of rage.

"You better take your crazy ass out of here." He snapped, using one arm to put the pregnant bitch behind his back.

"Is she pregnant with your baby?" I screamed. The thought of it driving me mad.

"Why the fuck you wanna know" he shouted more defensive than I've ever seen him. Tears began to well in my eyes.

"How the fuck you're ok with getting her ass pregnant but talked shit about wearing a condom with me? Huh, explain that shit to me?" I yelled in his direction. The girl tried to maneuver around him.

"Your ass better calm the fuck down." She snapped.

"Bitch don't talk to me, don't say shit to me. I will fuck you and that baby up." I threatened, rushing over in her direction. There was a crowd of people beginning to gather around but I didn't give a damn. I wanted to punch the girl in her face.

Just as I charged up a few stairs Raheim pushed me with enough force to knock me backwards. I fell down three stairs hitting my head on the railing. They both walked by me.

"Kelly I don't know how much clearer I can get. I don't want shit to do with your ass. Leave me alone." He emphasized the words leave me alone.

"That was supposed to be my baby, bitch. I better never see your ass on the street." I yelled at the girl, now walking confidently toward his car. My head was hurting and I didn't yet stand up but held my hand up to my head instead. I didn't have time to be embarrassed, the love of my damn life was walking away with a pregnant bitch.

Raheim sprang into action and ran over to where I sat on the ground. He reached his hand up to the back of my neck. The grip he had on me was enough to cause my shoulders to tense. His voice came in low and threatening.

"Threaten my girl or my baby again and I swear I'll kill your crazy ass myself. I didn't want your stupid ass cause you crazy as shit so step the fuck off. If I ever find out you touched her I'm coming for you." He shoved me hard, releasing my neck and leaving me speechless.

I wasn't sure what hurt more, seeing him walk away with another girl or him threatening to kill me. I stood up with a group of people watching. I reached for one of my heels that fell off when I tumbled down the stairs. "What the fuck are y'all looking at? Damn." I yelled at the crowd of people standing around.

Embarrassment start creeping in and I walked as quickly as I could back to my car. Tears threatening to pour from my eyes. *His ass is gonna be sorry* I promised myself.

I couldn't let him go because it meant what every other dude said was true. All of my ex's told me I was a good booty call but not much more. With Raheim chasing after and coming to see me I got to feel like I was more than a piece of ass. Now he was walking away with a bitch he got pregnant and treating me like I was a second class citizen. *Hell NO!* I shouted within myself.

Time to Talk

Janet

I still haven't gotten over the loss of Amir. Not having him come to visit these last two weeks have been hell but I've been making a few decisions. Being here for fifteen years meant I've heard more than my share of street dealings. Before I went under I used to rub shoulders with a guy named Jimmy. He was the biggest drug dealer this side of the Mississippi. He trusted me with most of his business until I left him for Carlos.

Jimmy was pissed but eventually he got over it when he saw that I got knocked up. He knew that I was useless to him now that I was having a baby. Didn't realize how useless I'd actually become. I remained loyal to Jimmy by keeping his secrets even though I've seen some pretty fucked up shit. A big part of me wanted Carlos because he wasn't into the streets, other than chasing anything in a skirt.

It was something intoxicating about being with the hottest looking dude in Philly. Within the first few weeks of my incarceration Jimmy had one of his women write me a letter saying I should have stayed with him. I was in luck as both Jimmy's girlfriend and daughter were incarcerated with me now. They were both arrested for drug trafficking and murder thrown in for good measure. This let me know that Jimmy was still in business. They rarely shared what got them here but occasionally I heard things. I made an appointment with my lawyer to discuss my options.

Raheim would regret turning his back on me. I would make sure of it. But first I need to get out of my current living nightmare.

Check Your Hoes

Felicia

I prolonged the inevitable conversation about who else Rah was seeing but after the crazy bitch in the parking lot tried to attack me I realized it was mandatory. The minute we were back in the car he looked both embarrassed and furious.

"Yo, Felicia." He started but I interrupted him.

"Listen, I've never had a problem with whatever you did before we were serious but things are different now. If you want me, it needs to be me Rah. We can't have crazy ass chicks trying to hurt me or the baby." I stared straight ahead.

"You know I would never let anybody hurt you right?" he asked. "I would kill somebody before I let them hurt you or the baby. You don't have to worry about that chick. I haven't talked to her since before the club incident but she's not trying to hear it. I'll handle it." He promised while pulling me into him for a kiss.

"Kiss me." He said with his lips barely touching mine. I pressed my lips into his for a quick kiss but his hand firmly held me closer.

"No, kiss me." He demanded. He was so sexy when he demanded affection. I pressed my lips into his before he began licking my bottom lip with his tongue. For a brief moment I forgot where we were. Nothing and nobody else mattered at the moment. I kissed him softly until my body became uncomfortable in my twisted position.

"We better pull off before Mall police stop us." I joked while pulling away.

"You're right, let's hit up Aunt Sadie. She made me lasagna yesterday." He stated. I've grown close to his aunt over the last few weeks and she treated me like I was her daughter.

"If her lasagna taste anything like that meatloaf she made the other day I'm in trouble." I responded.

It took us thirty minutes to get to his aunt's house. He pulled into a parking space and jumped out to open the door for me. I stepped out and pulled my black summer dress down over my hips.

"Where you at woman?" he shouted out as we walked into her house.

"I'm in the kitchen." She answered. I waddled behind him into the kitchen. It's funny how big my stomach seemed to get after Raheim found out I was pregnant.

"How are you?" Aunt Sadie stood up from her chair and kissed us both. She lingered in front of me to rub my stomach.

"Look at you girl, bout ready to bust." She said with a smile on her face. I laughed.

"We found out what we're having today." Raheim said proudly.

"Oh really? Please tell me it's a girl." She turned toward him with a smile on her face.

"Sorry, you didn't pray hard enough. We're having a baby boy." He said proudly while taking his seat at the table.

"You sound like your daddy. He was so proud to find out he was having a son. He couldn't stop telling everybody he was gonna be a dad." She said. I noticed the look of surprise register on Rah's face. "A boy huh? Now we can decorate. Felicia tell him to dig in his long pockets and pull out enough for two girls to go shopping." She held my hand and turned to look at him with a bit of excitement.

"I knew this was a bad idea. You see this Felicia? Come for lasagna and leave with empty pockets." He said with a smirk on his face.

"Well, you know lasagna ain't free in these here parts." She sashayed over to the fridge and took out an aluminum pan.

"You hungry too?" she asked as I took my seat.

"Yes ma'am we are." I rubbed my belly.

We continued to talk and I enjoyed the banter back and forth before Raheim filled her in on the episode at the Mall parking lot.

"You know what you gotta do don't you Raheim?" Aunt Sadie asked.

"I'm gonna handle it. I knew she was crazy but I didn't know she was that crazy." He stated. Just hearing him retell the story made me feel upset. After what happened to Amir I didn't want to take her threats lightly.

"Handle it how? You need to go get a restraining order for her crazy ass. I told your father the same thing about Janet. No offense but you have to be smart. She showed you she's crazy so you better believe her. Y'all are having a baby now. Think about it." His aunt schooled him on the seriousness of people's actions.

"You're right." I gave my two cents.

"Don't worry I'll handle it. Now tell me if you made one of your famous pies to go with this lasagna." He changed the subject using humor.

"I'm surprised your greedy ass ain't big as a damn house by now." She answered laughing. Though I was smiling I was silently worried. All I knew is that he better check his hoes before I have this baby.

Generational Curses

Raheim

Today was the first day my aunt Sadie compared me to my dad. It took me by surprise. She didn't have any dessert and just as we were ready to leave she called me upstairs.

"I'll be right back." I kissed Felicia on her forehead and passed her the television remote. I met my aunt inside her bedroom where she closed the door behind me.

"Look Raheim, I know we were all joking and having a good time but I really need you to be careful. I never told you this but your father was a playboy. He was so fine he couldn't walk outside without women gawking at him. Beauty is a blessing and a curse. But the problem with your father was that he never wanted to listen and it cost him his life." She reached for my hands.

Words caught in my throat. Losing Amir must have been on her mind.

"You have to think about Felicia and your son and you don't want history repeating itself." She continued.

"Why you ain't never tell me my dad was happy he was having me?" I asked curiously.

"I, I don't know. I thought your mom would have told you. Boy was he happy about you. I remember when he first came to tell me she was pregnant with you. You couldn't wipe the smile off his face if you paid him. When he told me it was by your mom." She paused. "Don't get me wrong. I wouldn't trade you or your brother in for the world but your mother was trouble from the start. He broke up with her a few times in front of me and she would go off. I've never seen anything like it until you told me what happened today. Watch your back and don't let pride stand in the way of doing what's right for you and your family." She finished talking.

"I'll handle it. Don't worry Aunt Sadie. I appreciate you telling me about my dad today. My mom made it seem like he didn't want nothing to do with us." I responded.

She pulled he hands away and looked at me with disbelief in her eyes.

"She told you what? Your dad was always asking to come get you and your brother. She would say it was ok just to get him to her house and when he didn't want to spend time with her she would kick him out. He used to have me ask to get y'all so that he could see you. Then she got hip to that and stopped letting you come with me. If your mom couldn't have him she wasn't letting anybody else have him including you and Amir." My Aunt filled me in.

"So what you saying is, all this time my dad wanted to be around but Janet gave him a hard time?" I asked incredulously. Janet was vindictive but I didn't realize how deranged her ass really was. What kind of woman does that shit to her own kids?

"I'll handle it tomorrow." I promised. She gave me a hug and whispered.

"That's what your father said but I need *you* to mean it."

I promised her again that I would before heading back downstairs to get Felicia. She stood up when I came down the stairs and gave my aunt a hug and kiss on the cheek. When we got back in the car Felicia looked my way.

"Is everything ok?" she asked.

"Yeah, she just wants us to be careful. She told me a few things I didn't know about my dad." I filled her in.

"Oh yeah, that's cool. Care to share?" she asked softly. What I loved about Felicia was that she always knew when I needed her.

"Janet always made us feel like my dad was a deadbeat but I just found out that he fought to get us. He wanted to spend that time and Janet's crazy ass wouldn't let him if it meant she couldn't be involved." I said staring off in front of me.

"Rah, you will never have to worry about me doing that to you." She reached over and touched my hand.

"I know cause I'm never leaving your ass." I promised. My cell started to ring and for a moment I wanted to ignore it. Another call from Kelly right now would definitely send me over the edge.

After the second ring I pulled it out of my pocket. Dre's name flashed on the screen.

"Hello?" I answered.

"About damn time. We need to talk. I found out about that chick at your brother's service." Dre spoke through the phone.

"Ok, where you gone be at in about an hour? I have Felicia with me but we're on our way back to her crib." I stated.

"Meet me over at the Woodland Ave spot." He answered. This must be important because he wanted to meet up with me now instead of telling me what he knew over the phone. "Cool, I'll be there." I ended the call.

"That was Dre. He wants to meet up with me for a little bit." I filled her in.

"Its ok, just drop me off at the house. Are you coming back tonight?" she asked with understanding.

"Yeah, I'll be there." I promised.

"Just be careful please." She turned to look me in the eye.

"I will be babe." I drove her over to her house on Cedar Ave and waited for her to open the door and go inside before I pulled off. I sped off in the direction of Woodland Ave thinking about how I was going to have to handle my Kelly problem.

Dre and a few of his boys were already standing outside on the front porch. I parked and jumped out.

"Rah, what up my nigga?" Tim, an old friend from high school asked. I jogged up the stairs and shook everyone's hand.

"How you doin fellas?" I turned to look at Dre who was pretty quiet.

"We'll be back." Dre stated before heading toward the house. I followed close behind. Candy was laying on the couch texting.

Dre didn't start talking until after we walked in the room.

"We got the girl." He said in my direction. My heart sped up.

"What do you mean you got her?" I asked

"My boy Tim and his crew picked her up about two hours ago." He informed me.

"Where she at? You sure it was her?" I asked fully aware of the magnitude of the situation.

"Yeah, we sure. She confessed to being there but said she wasn't going to say nothing. I don't trust that bitch. I can handle it but I thought you might want to do it yourself." Dre's tone was all business. I understood fully what he was trying to say.

"Naw, take me to her." I said. Before we end her life I needed to know how involved she was in my brother's death.

"Cool. Let's ride." Dre walked back out of the room and down the stairs.

"Candy get your ass up and make me something to eat. I'll be back in a minute." Dre threw that over his shoulder.

"C'mon we out." Dre, Tim and his boys and I headed to his car and hopped in. This felt too familiar. The last time we were all in a car together was to rescue my brother. I shook the feeling out of my head. He headed toward his North Philly house.

"That bitch is hot, too bad she gotta get smoked." Tim said lighting up a cigarette.

"Maybe we can have a little bit of fun wit her first." One of Tim's boys said, rubbing the crotch of his pants with anticipation.

"It's your call. Cause if you ask me, we should go in and blast that bitch." He said angrily.

"I want to ask a few questions first." I said quietly. She is one of the last people to see my brother alive and I wanted to know what she knew. We pulled into a park out front of one of his North Philly houses. It was just as ordinary as the rest of the houses on the block. Nothing stood out about it. We all filed into the house and my heart nearly pounded out of my chest.

"She's in the basement." Dre said leading the way. I wasn't sure what to expect when we got down there but the first thing I noticed was a big roll of plastic wrap propped against the wall and a large bag of cement beside it. Off in the far corner was a broken section of concrete.

My eyes finally fell upon the pretty cinnamon colored woman with strands of sweaty locks falling into her wide eyes. She looked scared, with her wrists taped in front of her. Her mouth was taped shut by electrical tape. Tim and his friends stood around her in a circle.

"She's too pretty to waste." Tim's boy stated.

"I want to talk to her alone." I said, my eyes never leaving her face.

"We'll be upstairs." Dre said before signaling his boys to follow him back up the steps.

I waited to speak until after I heard the basement door close. Every emotion imaginable ran through me.

"I want you to know that my boys are planning on killing you but I can save you. When I move the tape you better not scream, do you hear me?" I asked, searching her eyes for any sign of deception. She nodded her head desperately. I needed her to trust me but I wasn't there to be nice. I slowly ripped the tape from her mouth. She didn't scream.

"I need to ask you a few questions and I swear if you lie to me your ass is going to end up apart of this floor. She glanced around the basement with tears overflowing.

"Okay." Her voice came out low and afraid.

"How did you know my brother?" I asked, curious to hear her answer. Amir wasn't the type of kid who had multiple women.

"Jackie told me about what you did to Showboat. She wanted to pay you back so she asked me to get Amir's attention. They didn't say anything about killing him." She choked on her words.

"Did they pay you?" I asked. Her head dropped.

"Did they fucking pay you?" I shouted at her. She nodded her head yes.

"How much?" I asked, now inches away from her face.

"Five thousand, I was only supposed to get him to trust me until they grabbed him but Boom demanded I stay to take care of him." She offered up information. She didn't have anyone to protect they were all killed in the warehouse that night.

"Have you talked to anyone?" I asked.

"No."

"You sure?"

"Yes, I'm sure." She pleaded.

"Good." I stated before standing up straight. I didn't need to know anymore. She took money to trap my brother and she claims no one else knows. I walked toward the stairs.

"What's going to happen to me now?" she asked with obvious panic.

"They'll set you free." I said nonchalantly.

"Yo Dre." I shouted from the bottom of the steps.

Dre and Tim came running down the stairs.

"What's your move my man?" Dre asked. With one look I gave a small nod. I promised that everyone involved in what happened to Amir would pay and she was no different. Tim shot into action grabbing the roll of plastic and spreading it across the floor around her chair. Her eyes grew wide and she began to plead.

"Please, I didn't mean for this to happen? I cared about your brother. I really did." She begged through sobs.

"Really bitch? You cared enough to trap his ass didn't you?" Dre asked walking up to her and slapping her hard across the face. She screamed. I heard Tim dragging a heavy bucket of cement across the floor. When I turned in his direction I noticed the long wooden table with an electric saw resting on the table top.

"Oh my God! Please don't do this." She screamed.

"Where's the tape, her ass is too loud." Dre walked over to the table and grabbed the silver electrical tape and tore a piece of it off before aggressively putting it across her mouth. She mumbled and groaned through the tape.

My heart didn't change, I wanted her dead. If she would have put her foot down before she would have been safe now. Tim covered the table in plastic. Dre lifted her from the chair but she moved around furiously before trying to speak through the tape.

"She got last words." Dre smirked.

"Alright, let her talk." I said. He ripped the tape from her face causing her to scream.

"Please don't do this. Just give me a minute. Please." She squirmed. Her tears rolled then fell onto her collarbone.

Tim pulled the girl down on the table while Dre wrapped her by the ankles with the tape. Tim's hands squeezed both her tits as Dre reached into his pants and pulled out his .45 with a silencer on the end. Her eyes grew wider than saucers. Dre raised his hand slowly but she screamed out.

"Wait, I'm pregnant!" she screamed.

"Hold up." I raised my hand to stop Dre from shooting. My mind started to race. Do I kill her or let her live?

"By who?" I snapped.

"By Amir. We had sex a few times." She confessed. She had to be lying. Amir was a virgin. Besides, he was waiting to be married before he went there.

"You lying piece of shit. Why would you fucking lie on that? Amir was a virgin" I asked in disbelief.

"I swear. I was taking care of him and I made him sleep with me. His arms were tied behind him so he couldn't stop me but we did have sex." She continued to confess.

"So what you're saying is that kidnapping him wasn't enough but raping felt just about right?" I walked over to her and grabbed her by the hair.

"If your ass is lying I'm gonna fucking kill you myself." I threatened. She winced in pain but whispered.

"It's true, I swear."

"Tim send ya man out for a pregnancy test real quick." Dre ordered. Tim moved quickly up the stairs. She closed her eyes in what looked like prayer, which made me think of how Amir must have felt the entire time he was held hostage. Well this time it would be on her.

There was an awkward silence as we all waited for Tim's boy to come back from the pharmacy. Tim wouldn't stop rubbing her boobs and reaching down to grab her crotch. A million thoughts raced in my head. If she was pregnant I would have to let her live so I could have my brother's child. The front door opening and closing let us know he was back. Seconds later his heavy footsteps filled the basement as he brought us the pregnancy test.

"Pee on this." Dre unwrapped the test and held it out to her.

"My hands." She held her tied wrist out.

"We'll hold you up. Grab her and put her over that bucket." Dre barked orders. They both helped her by holding her in a seated position of the bucket. She looked humiliated as Dre held the stick under her ass while she peed on the pregnancy stick. Once she was done, Dre handed me the stick to hold as they lifted her back up to the table. I remembered Felicia and wondered if she took one of these to find out about our baby.

I owed it to my brother to find out if this broad really was having his baby. We waited for ten minutes before looking at the results. Dre picked it up and passed it to me without looking. I was nervous and my palms started to sweat. The test showed a negative blue line, which meant the bitch lied. Without thinking I reached for the gun, aimed at her head and pulled the trigger. The air grew quiet as I stood frozen for a moment. Dre grabbed the gun with a cloth and began rubbing my prints off.

"Go home Rah, we got this." He said tossing me his car keys.

"Tell Tim's boy to drop you off over Woodland Ave for your whip and drive my car back. I walked up the stairs like he said but there was something different about me now. Though I have been called some of everything under the sun, I was never called a murderer, until tonight.

I've Got Your Back

Felicia

After being dropped off at home I took a nap before I decided to finally call my mother to tell her about the baby. She was super religious which is why I waited this long. Knowing she was a few states over in Georgia made me feel a bit better though. I tried the house phone first, it rang three times before she finally answered.

"Felicia?" her voice came out happy, making my news that much more difficult.

"Hey mama, how are you?" I started.

"Much better now. It feels like forever since I've talked to you last. What you been up to?" she asked casually.

My mother and I have a complicated relationship. Growing up I was her favorite until I decided to move out on my own. She made me feel like I wouldn't make it in the world without being under her roof. Our relationship has been strained ever since and my big sister has avoided me also. It bordered the lines of an occult where my mother perceived the world as a threat and her house as the only safe place. Needless to say mental illness was a major factor. However, it also helped me to understand Raheim and the relationship he has with his own mother.

"It has been a while. I'm doing ok though. How about you mama? Are you ok?" I asked to gauge how she was feeling.

"Well, your sister is trying to go to this fancy school to study law. I keep telling her that the devil's playground ain't no place for my girls but she doesn't want to listen. She's starting to act like you." She finished her thought off. *Good for her!* I thought to myself.

"She needs to find her own way is all mama. I have some good news!" I tried to sound excited. It wouldn't help but it gave me some false confidence.

"I need some good news right about now." She said in her 'tired of being sad' voice.

"You're gonna be a grandma." I said the words with enough enthusiasm to sell a used car.

"When did you get married? Why weren't we invited?" she started throwing out questions designed to make me feel ashamed.

"Mama, I'm."

"I know you don't like being around us now that you done got all high siddity but it would've been nice to receive an invitation to your wedding." She cut me off.

"But listen." I interrupted her but Rah walked in.

"Mom, I gotta go but I'll call you later ok?" I ended the call before she could answer. That is pretty much how my life went with my mother.

"Babe where you at?" Rah shouted out.

"Here." I waddled toward the living room. He had a serious expression on his face.

"What's the matter?" I asked walking closer to him and wrapping my arms around his waist.

"Nothing, I need to take a shower. I feel sweaty." He said looking down at me. For a moment our eyes locked and I remembered how he couldn't look me in the face not too long ago. He broke our stare first by pushing me back enough to walk by me. Something was wrong, I could sense it.

"I have clean towels in the bathroom and you left a bag with changing clothes upstairs in my room." I pointed toward the ceiling

"Our bedroom." He corrected. Though he made me smile I knew that something serious was going on under the surface. Whatever Rah did when he left me had him twisted.

He walked upstairs and headed for the bathroom. I decided that I would wait until he was done to seduce his ass into talking. He didn't press me for sex since we've

been back from Jamaica but I didn't need him feeling like
he needed someone else to fulfill that need. Pregnant or not
his ass was getting it tonight. It wasn't until I heard him in
the shower that I knew something was wrong.

"Shit!" I heard him shout. I walked over to the
stairwell.

"I'm fucking sorry. Amir I'm sorry." I heard him
hitting the shower wall. I walked as quickly as I could up
the stairs and into the unlocked bathroom.

"Rah are you ok?" I asked. He was crying as he leaned
against the shower wall.

"I fucking killed my brother. I did that shit." He was
yelling between his tears.

"Raheim, it's not your fault. Listen to me." I tried to
calm him.

"That fucking night at the club, I was trying to prove
that I was a man so that dude would know not to fuck with
me. I should have walked away." I kicked off my shoes and

pulled the shower curtain back. Getting my clothes wet was the least of my worries. He needed me now. This was the first time since Amir's funeral that I've seen Raheim break down like this. I stepped into the tub and gave him a hug. My swollen belly pressing into his lower back. We both stood there for a second, water beating down on our backs, in silence. After the moment passed I reached for my loofa and scented body wash and poured just enough to make it sudsy. Raheim stood quietly as I began to softly and slowly wash his back.

I hoped he read my metaphor. I am and will always be his backbone. I have his back and nothing from here on out could change that. Once I was done he slowly turned to face me. He stepped around me making sure not to make me fall. He pressed my back against the wall, the warm water now rinsing him.

"I love you Felicia." He whispered while leaning down to kiss me softly. This was so different from a few months ago. Before he couldn't stand to look me directly in the eye while being intimate. But now he spoke the words love without blinking.

"I'm in love with you too Raheim." He held my gaze as we silently promised to be here for one another. His hands reached up and slowly massaged my breast as our lips pressed together erotically. He began pulling my dress up over my head. It was now soaking wet, he threw it onto the bathroom floor. His hands hungrily unfastened my bra, releasing my fuller breast. There was something about this pregnancy that made my body more sensitive. I kissed at his mouth as he tried to pull my panties down.

Raheim dropped to his knees, water now hitting against my chest and rolling to the tips of my nipples where they poured down onto his forehead. He finished working my panties down over my legs until I was carefully stepping out of them. He helped me lift one leg up on the side of the tub as he pressed his face close to my belly. He planted kisses on our unborn child before his lips wandered to my lower region. It's been weeks since he's touched me there and I shuddered. I felt his lips press against my clit causing me to close my eyes. He spread my lips with his own before pulling me into his mouth where he sucked softly. I reached down and held his head in place as moans escaped from my throat. His hands reached upward holding my stomach for a few seconds before reaching for both my nipples.

"Yesss." I moaned softly. He was going to make my knees weak. His tongue was making circles before flicking quickly across my hot spot.

"Oh, Raheim." I spoke barely able to contain myself. I wanted him badly though I was afraid of falling.

"Let's go into the room." I whispered. He looked up into my eyes, never taking his mouth off of me. I could barely see his face over my belly. He stood carefully before reaching out of the shower to grab a towel. My bathroom floor was covered with slip resistant mats.

He allowed me to step out of the shower first before following me to our bedroom. I planned on lying on my back he stopped me by turning me around to face him. He kissed my lips down to my neck before bending just enough to suck my nipple. Both harder than usual. I rubbed his back with each stroke of his tongue. Just as the feeling threatened to overtake me he stood up straight, walked to the bed and lay on his back. His dick now standing at full attention. He reached up for me. I held his hands while straddling him. Easing down on his hardness until I felt every inch of him inside of me. He held me in place for a moment before moving his hips slowly up and down.

As crazy as this might sound it felt beautiful, this moment felt beautiful. My fear of never being with Raheim again because of being pregnant scared me but now I'm making love to my soulmate while carrying his child. I bit the inside of my lip to stop from crying as I worked my hips to his rhythm. He stared up at me with an emotion I've never seen before. He was in love and it was clearly written across his face. I smiled down at him as he reached up, grabbing both my breast as he moved faster and faster. He didn't flinch or turn away from me. I broke our stare down first when I threw my head back and moaned. He was stroking my g-spot and I was close to an orgasm.

"Cum for me." He spoke lightly. I rolled my head back and enjoyed the sensation as he continued to rock us both. "Cum for me, that's it." I bounced harder on his lap as we both were close to reaching an orgasm. When I could no longer take it I let out a guttural moan that provoked Raheim to reach his own personal sweet spot.

"Shit! I'm cumming." We both sang out in unison. When it was over I dropped down beside him. We both lay staring up at the ceiling before he turned to lay his head on my belly.

I stroked his hair as he listened to our baby's heartbeat.

Can't Get Away With It

Kelly

It wasn't until I got home that I realized how embarrassed and angry I was. He damn near took my head off anytime I acted like he didn't have to wear protection. So seeing another bitch pregnant with his baby threw me through a few different loops. What hurt the most though was how he treated me like I didn't mean shit. I've been with Raheim for over two years and we were only allowed to see each other once a damn week. I needed to be with him. He doesn't realize how many dudes I passed up to be with him and now he tosses me away like trash. Well, it wasn't gonna happen.

I couldn't tell none of my girls about what was going on because they all thought Raheim was wrapped around my finger. If I couldn't have his baby no one would. I had something for both their asses and he better hope I don't see them before she has that damn baby. There was nothing inside of me that said quit and because of that I can't let

him get away with it.

Time to Talk

Janet

After speaking with my attorney she informed me that we may be able to make a deal. She also said there is no turning back once I go down this road. I wasn't worried about turning back but if I could actually get out was of more concern. She told me I needed to start working on my behavior so that it would look good on my record. Outside of the occasional outburst I was doing pretty good.

Like always I stayed pretty far away from Jimmy's people. The last thing I want to do is raise any suspicion. I was sitting in my cell when my cellmate walked in.

"We got next on TV you coming?" she asked.

"Nah, I don't feel much like being around people about now." I stated dryly.

"Okay, well feel better ok?" she asked rhetorically. No one knows what to say when you lose someone but especially when you lose a kid.

I laid back on the bed and thought about getting some dick. It's funny how much you miss it when you ain't getting it. Like always I pictured being in bed with Carlos *Ah Papi, why'd you have to be such an ass?* I said to myself. Not having Carlos on the outside would be hard but my sole mission of getting out would be to force my son to love me again. I needed Raheim to love me to make amends for what I've done with Carlos. I was going to give the D.A everything I had on Jimmy, which I knew was enough to put his ass away for life. I knew where he stored his money, his product and more than a few dead bodies. He was a sadistic bastard with a wicked sense of humor. For now I would sit quiet, blend with the inmates until it was my time to talk. Then I'd sing like a muthafuckin canary.

Real Talk

Raheim

Knowing what I did had me wanting to flee the city but I couldn't just up and go with Felicia hitting close to eight and a half months pregnant. I owned a few houses in Miami and Atlanta but they all had tenants. I used my money wisely and kept a few off shore accounts in case I was ever in a jam. My nerves were still on edge after shooting the girl known as Pam a week ago but Felicia has been doing a good job of keeping me calm.

"Babe, I have to head out to handle some business real quick but I'll be back in about four hours."

"Ok. Rah, be careful." She said trying to stand up from the couch.

"Don't get up. When I come back I'll rub your feet for you." I offered. Her ankles were starting to swell and even though she thought she was gaining a lot of weight it looked good on her. How could I not be in love with a woman willing to transform her body to give my child life? The more I thought about having this baby the more I fell in love with them both. I leaned over and kissed her on the lips before heading out of my apartment door. We needed to have a real discussion about where we planned on staying after having the baby is born. We still haven't done anything for the baby yet.

The business I had to handle was meeting Mia and Alexis at our usual spot in Atlantic City. Things have been running on autopilot but we always meet up every few weeks to make sure all is well in business. I entered my suite to find they were both scantily dressed waiting.

"What's up Raheim?" Mia asked first.

"Hey. Nothing much is up. How you feel?" I sent a question back. Alexis undressed me with her eyes. Not that I couldn't blame her I was wearing one of my favorite pair of jeans and a bright white Michael Kors button down. My watch was shining super bright and Felicia convinced me to cut my long braids down to a low curly top. It didn't take much convincing but I figured if I'm about to be a dad I should grow up a little bit.

"You look different, good though." Alexis complimented.

"Well you both look sexy as always." I walked over to the bar and poured myself a glass of rum and headed for the fridge to mix it with coke.

"How's work?" I asked casually.

"I'm straight but my cousin wants to be put on." Mia stated before turning around completely to face me.

"You know we can't do that Mia. Too many people can fuck things up. I thought we said not to go telling people what the fuck you doing." My voice was threatening.

"Relax, I didn't tell her how we operate. She is attracted to my lifestyle so I said I would see what I can do." She explained.

"Are you willing to share your clients?" I asked already sure of the answer.

"Hell no!" she snapped.

"Well she can come on when you are." I responded taking a sip from my glass. She got my point. Putting myself on the line was never an option. Any girl I put on understand that if she crossed me she would be the person to pay the price. I'm the middle man.

"We haven't heard from you in a few weeks, what's going on?" Alexis asked lying back on the luxurious sofa in the living room area of our suite.

"I had some business in Jamaica for a few weeks. I'm also about to be a dad." I said proudly. Both girls looked at one another with alarm.

"A baby? How is that going to affect my bottom line?" Mia asked getting straight to business.

"I don't have any plans to change anything right now. We'll keep doing what we've been doing.

"How we know your ass ain't going to change your mind once you see the damn child? Especially if it's a girl." Alexis added her two cents.

"Because I gotta make a living to support the child so stop fucking stressing and just keep hooking up with your clients and leave the rest to me." I raised my voice.

We wrapped up our business an hour later and I headed back home. After being committed to Felicia for a little while I realized that she is the only female in my life aside from my aunt Sadie that doesn't stress or nag me to death. After the incident with Kelly I changed my number but not before calling each of my other girls to tell them I wouldn't be coming to see them anymore. A few of them already got the message when I was a no show from the Jamaica trip. A few cursed me to my grave and a few cried and acted like I told them I was going off to Iraq.

For the first time in my entire adult life I'm only seeing one woman. Felicia was reading an Essence

Magazine when I walked in so I tossed my keys on the sofa table.

"You ready for your massage?" I asked while sitting down beside her on the couch and lifting her feet to my lap. She moaned, anticipating relaxation.

"We need to talk. I've always been honest with you but now that you're my girl you need to know a few things about me." I started. She lowered the magazine and put all eyes on me.

"What is it?" she asked cautiously.

"Relax, it's nothing like that." I stated knowing she immediately thought of other women.

"I gotta be honest, I've never told anyone this and it makes me nervous now. I've never told you how I make my money and I appreciate that you've never asked." She shifted some more in her seat with an obvious question mark on her face.

"I connect corporate executives, business owners and millionaires with beautiful women to act out their crazy ass sexual fantasies. My cut is taken from their weekly payments." I finished talking without looking her way. She stared at me for a minute before laughter erupted from her throat.

"Are you serious?" she asked after her laughing spell.

"Dead ass serious. Why you laughing?" I asked, a little offended that she wasn't taking me seriously.

"Because I thought you were about to say you were a drug dealer. I don't care how you make your money Rah. Long as your ass is careful we're good." She said it like she wasn't freaked out about what I did.

"So you not mad?" I asked. One of the reasons I never told her was because of the reaction I thought she'd have.

"Why would I be mad, you haven't brought home any drama other than the dick whipped chick from the mall." She explained.

"I don't know how much longer I'm gonna be in the business though. I'm not trying to put you and the baby in the middle of anymore bullshit." I confessed. A few of my connections helped me invest my money in a few different ventures and businesses, which cleaned up my money.

"I'm here for you so no matter what you do I'm fine with it." She confirmed what I already knew.

"Which house you wanna stay in after we have the baby?" I asked, changing the subject. She flexed her toes as I continued to massage her feet.

"I don't care where we stay as long as I get to be with you." She said. Her words hit me in a place never touched by anyone.

"Alright then." I said attempting to stand up. I was hungry and she made my dick hard and I knew sex at the moment wasn't going to be possible.

She started something that I planned on finishing.

Labor Pains

Felicia

Both Raheim and I have been living a fairytale existence for the last few weeks. A big part of it was avoiding the fact that he lost his brother and that we were about to become parents whether we are ready or not. Now that I am down to my last few weeks I've been trying to stay off my feet as much as possible. That is until the doctor told me I could help my labor along by walking. A few nights Rah drove us over to a local park and we walked around the track. He's been better than patient with me and I can't say that it's been easy but he's obliged each of my outrageous cravings no matter what time of day or not.

Last night was really special though. Rah spoke directly into my belly and the baby continued to kick and move around. Raheim was just as fascinated as I was. He made me record my belly moving with each kick. Today he left me in the house alone to go meet up with Dre so I decided to take a walk to the corner store. I threw on a pair of black tights and one of Raheim's t-shirts. More because I loved how he smelled and also it was the only shirt big enough to pull down over my belly.

Walking slowly down the front stairs to my house I waved to a few of my neighbors. The baby was weighing heavy on my bladder but I managed to waddle to the store. A few young guys were there grabbing bags of chips for what I was sure was the munchies. They both smelled like weed strong enough to make me feel like gagging. I grabbed a cranberry juice from the freezer and walked toward the back to see what type of snacks I wanted from there.

"No I'm gonna say something to the bitch." I heard from a female voice behind me. I didn't turn to see who it was.

"Hey you." The voice persisted. I turned to see who it was coming from. My heart stopped when I saw the same girl from the Mall standing there with an 'I'm gonna fuck you up' face. Not that I was scared of her but I couldn't risk fighting while I was damn near nine months pregnant.

"Yes." I answered calmly.

"Ain't you the chick that was with Raheim the other day at the Mall?" she asked with a ratchet tone. I looked over her shoulder before answering. Another girl was standing behind her ready to instigate or get some shit started.

"Who is asking?" I answered just as sarcastic. I turned left and right to see what I could grab that would hurt her if something jumped off. There were a few glass jars within arm's reach on the shelf.

"Bitch you don't have to get smart, I just wanted to ask you a few questions." She responded.

"What makes you think I have to answer any of your damn questions? Move out of my way." I tried to walk by but she blocked me.

"Well did you know that I was with Raheim for two years?" she tried to do a typical ghetto girl move.

"Good for you, now get outta my way right now." I snapped.

"Bitch, the only reason he with you now is because he's mad at me but he'll be back." She snapped, using her finger to poke me in the shoulder.

"Put your hands on me again and we gone have a problem." I warned. Though I was being brave I was secretly hoping someone would come back to break things up. For the first time in a long time I had someone else to think about.

"What the fuck you gone do? I will whip your pregnant ass up in this store." She threatened, elevating her voice.

"Yeah, whatever." I rolled my eyes and walked toward the door, which meant I needed to turn my back.

The light skinned chick's friend held out her foot, tripping me and making me lose my balance. I fell to the floor, using both my arms to shield my stomach from hitting the floor. With every ounce of rage I could muster I reached for a glass jar and threw at the girl who tripped me. In one flash I saw both girls reach down for my hair and started to pull and the trick who was infatuated with Raheim tried to kick me hard in the stomach but only got my arm.

"Yo, what the fuck!" one of the guys who smelled like weed said. Both girls were pulling on me and kicking me near my stomach. As best I could I shielded my belly, trying to protect my baby.

"Yo, she pregnant, y'all bitches is grimy as fuck." The guy said with a nervous laugh. He grabbed one of the girls and pulled her off me. The store owner started yelling that she was calling for the police. The guy reached to grab the girl who remained, she was punching me on my arms and the side of my head. When the store owner yelled he was calling for the police both girls ran out of the store.

I didn't have time to cry or feel any pain. The only thing I could think of was my baby.

"You alright? Here." He held out his hand and helped me up.

"Yeah, I'm fine." I said while trying to stand. A sharp pain shot up the side of my stomach.

"Ouch, damn!" I yelled out.

"Yo, call a fucking ambulance or some shit. They fucked her up. She bleeding and shit." He said frantically to the store owner. A few shoppers walked toward me to be nosey. The moment he said I was bleeding I thought it must be from my lip or scalp but when I looked down there was a small pool of blood on the floor between my legs.

I started to faint but the guy caught me.

"Move back give her some air. Let her sit on those crates." A few girls grabbed two empty crates by the counter and I took a seat. *I gotta call Rah* was the first thing to pop in my head. I reached inside my handbag and grabbed my cellphone. His phone rang four times before he finally answered.

"I'm on my way to the hospital." I said, wincing with pain.

"What? You alright? Are you in labor?" He shouted through the phone.

"I don't know, I was jumped by your little groupie and one of her friends, now I'm bleeding." The other end of the receiver went silent for a moment like the line went dead.

Now He'll Understand

Kelly

I would have continued to beat her ass had the guy not stopped me. Maybe now Raheim will come over to my house. He left me with no choice but to go off on his baby mom when he changed his damn cell number. It was by total accident I saw her go into the store. I was happy my girl Shay was with me cause she was always down for whatever. She was the only person I explained what happened to. I didn't give her all the details just that I saw Raheim with a pregnant bitch at the Mall and that he pushed me down the stairs when I confronted him.

We sat in my car and waited to see what happened next. The sound of sirens were heard in the distance.

"Your ass better get the fuck outta here before they arrest our asses." Shay chimed in. She fidgeted in her seat, filled with nervous energy.

"I'm leaving, I just want to know if they really called the cops. I pressed my luck, waiting to see if the sirens really did belong to the police. I didn't feel good about pulling off until I spotted the oversized red and white ambulance pulling up in front of the store's entrance. People were beginning to gather. *I hope her and her damn baby die.* I thought to myself.

No Threat, a Promise

Raheim

"Where are you?" I snapped back into reality.

"The ambulance is here, I'm going to University of Penn. Ouch" Felicia answered. My head started spinning. I knew Kelly was crazy but I didn't know how far she was willing to go.

"I'll meet you there." I ended the call.

"Everything cool man?" Dre asked looking in my direction.

"Crazy ass Kelly just jumped Felicia. She's on her way to the hospital now." I said standing up from the chair I was in.

"Oh shit! Go handle your business man. Hit me up later." Dre stood up and extended his hand for a handshake.

If it's not one thing it's something else. I couldn't deal with another lost and I swear if something is wrong with my baby I'm gonna kill that bitch. I jumped in my car and headed toward the hospital. I hit my Aunt Sadie's number on my phone.

"Hello?" she answered.

"Aunt Sadie, I'm headed over to the hospital." I said, not sure if I could tell her about Kelly. She already told me to handle it and though I thought changing my number was enough it obviously wasn't.

"What? Is Felicia having the baby." She asked excited.

"I'm not really sure. The girl I told you about had her jumped." I sucked it up and told her.
"Oh my God! What hospital is she going to?" she asked noticeably stirred to action.

"University of Penn. I'm on my way now." I filled her. I was trying to play it cool but I was nervous as shit.

"Ok, I'm coming now." She said before ending the call. When I changed my number I delete everyone's number except Felicia's, Mia and Alexis, Dre and my Aunt's. Everyone else wasn't relevant.

I didn't need Kelly's number though I know where she lives. Tonight she was going to see a side of me her ass haven't seen before. I drove as quickly to the hospital as I could, fighting back feelings of deja vue as I went. As always the hospital parking lot was overcrowded. I pulled in just as the ambulance holding Felicia arrived. I stopped to watch them lower her out on a stretcher. The white sheets were covered in blood between her legs.

"Damn what happened?" I asked walking quickly beside her stretcher. EMT's and paramedics walked her quickly into the ER and bypassed all of the sign in process. *This shit must be serious* I said to myself. Blood rushed to my ears as my heart pumped faster and faster. I thought of a thousand ways to kill Kelly if something happens to my kid.

"Where are they going to take her?" I asked the nurse at reception.

"Are you her husband?" the nurse asked.

"Uh no, I'm the child's father. She's my girlfriend." I answered.

"Ok, I'll go check for you, in the meantime please fill this out and I'll be right back." She passed me clipboard and I filled out as much information as I could. Aunt Sadie rushed in through the double doors and rushed up to me.

"What's going on?" she asked, worry written all across her face.

"I'm not really sure yet. No one is telling me shit and it's driving me mad. All Felicia told me is that the chick Kelly and another chick jumped her and that's she was bleeding. I saw her get out of the ambulance on a stretcher and she had blood everywhere but that's it." I explained what I knew.

An hour later the nurse approached me and let me know I was free to go to the back where they had Felicia. Me and my aunt bolted toward her room. I could hear her asking for me when we walked up.

"Raheim." She said with tears in her eyes.

"I'm here." I said, walking up to the edge of her bed.

"What did the doctor say?" I asked.

"They're going to keep me connected to the monitors. The baby appears to be ok but they said the bleeding is from placental abruption. The fight provoked it." She explained.

"What happened?" Aunt Sadie asking pulling us both up a chair.

"When you left I decided to walk to the store to get a few snacks and to help the baby drop. But when I got there that chick and her girl was following me. She had the damn nerve to say she wanted to ask me a few questions about my relationship with you. When I tried to walk away her friend tripped me and made me fall and they both attacked. I tried to protect my stomach as much as I could but her trifling ass was trying to kick me hard in the stomach."

It was hard sitting there listening to that. I was ready to hunt Kelly's ass down. It took everything inside of me to not jump up to leave.

"Oh my God!" Aunt Sadie said reaching out to hold her hand.

We set with her for another hour and got confirmation that she is ok but the doctor's want to hold her for a few days to monitor her.

"I'll be back." I stood up and leaned over to kiss her on the forehead.

"Aunt Sadie can you sit with her for a little bit? I have to handle something and I'll be right back." I gave my aunt a knowing stare. She nodded her head yes and turned back to face Felicia.

I walked back to my car on a mission. The ride back to Kelly's apartment took me about twenty five minutes. I got out after parking and hit the buzzer, waiting for an answer.

"Who is it?" her voice came on the loud speaker.

"It's Raheim." I said calmly.

"I knew you'd come." She said happily like she thought this was a social visit.

"Buzz me up." I said, controlling the anger that threatened to spill out of my throat. One second later the familiar buzzing unlocked the door and I walked on threw. I took the stairs and turned the door knob when I reached her apartment. It was already unlocked.

Kelly stood in the middle of the room completely naked except for a pair of red stilettos. *This bitch done really lost her damn mind.* I said to myself. I needed to play it off until I got closer to her.

"I knew you would come to your senses." She said with a sly smile on her face. I closed and locked the door behind me. I walked over to her like a man on a mission and grabbed her by the back of the neck and dragged her into the bathroom.

"Raheim what are you doing. You're hurting me." She screamed. When we got to the bathroom I threw her down on the floor and closed the bathroom door. I turned the sink and then the shower to drown out any noise and hit the on switch to her radio sitting on the countertop. Before I spoke I turned up the music. Her eyes were huge with fear.

My hand went up high and came down hard. She put her hand up to her face in shock.

"You like hitting pregnant chicks huh?" I asked, standing over her.

"You changed your phone number, what else was I supposed to do to get your attention?" she asked still holding her face.

"If something happens to my kid I will fucking kill you. Do you fucking get that?" I yelled.

"Why can she have your baby?" she spoke through cries.

I grabbed Kelly by the hair and pulled her up to her feet.

"Bitch, why the fuck don't you understand I don't want you? Huh? Why the fuck is that so hard to get through your thick ass skull?" I stared her down waiting for an answer. She only winced at my words before her eyes got teary eyed.

"Why were you fucking me for two years then Raheim? If you didn't have any intention on being wit me." She asked with rage in her voice despite the fact that I was pinning her down.

"If something is wrong with my baby your ass better move out of town or I'm gonna send your ass to your maker. This is the last time I tell you this. I don't want shit to do with your crazy ass. Nothing, we will never be together and I will never come here to fuck you. Now leave me the fuck alone." I yelled in her face before shoving her against the wall.

"Are you threatening me?" She asked in disbelief.

"No bitch I'm promising you." I answered before turning to leave. She reached for the radio, ripping the cord for the socket and threw it at my back. Without thinking I spun around and punched her hard enough to make her fall.

It wasn't until this moment I realized my mother was my father's Kelly.

Big Decisions

Raheim

Leaving Kelly's apartment made me realize how close I was to actually killing her. She refused to get the message no matter how loud I said it. The doctor's said they wanted to keep Felicia for observation and that was all I was giving Kelly. I used my shirt to wipe my prints off her door handles, both the bathroom and the front door before I left so I felt confident.

I hated realizing that my life was turning out to look the same as my folks. A newfound respect for my father was growing. If my mom is as crazy as Aunt Sadie is saying than my dad was trying to get away from her ass. A strong desire to hear the truth was growing inside of me. Another desire was slowly creeping in also. I wanted to be with Felicia permanently. I've never felt the need to protect anyone like I did her. I've told her about the worst parts of me and she was still around. She didn't change her mind about me, judge me or make me feel like shit. In the words of my boy Dre 'You need to get you one ride or die and leave them other birds alone.' I already knew that my kid was going to get the best of me and I vowed to never make them feel abandoned the way I was my mom.

I made my way back up to the hospital and went into Felicia's room where she was sleep and my Aunt Sadie was watching a Lifetime movie.

"Everything ok?" I whispered.

"She's stable so that's a good thing. Let me talk to you out here for a minute." She said while standing up and walking toward the door.

"Raheim this could have been serious." She started in on me when we got to the hallway.

"Yeah I know. I told the bitch to leave me alone, I changed my number and she still acting crazy." I explained.

"Well now it's time to include the law. She assaulted a pregnant woman that means she has no boundaries. You better thank God she didn't lose the baby." My aunt drove her point home.

"Yeah I know." I answered. I couldn't go to the police because I wanted to remain under the radar. My line of business wasn't exactly legit.

"I'm working on something, don't worry ok? We'll all be safe. I just need a little bit of time." I tried to reassure her. She kissed me on the cheek.

"I'm gonna go on home but tell Felicia I'll be back tomorrow ok?" she asked.

"Ok, I'll let her know." I said before walking back into her room.

I flipped the small, wall-mounted television off using the remote and took a seat by the bed. I watched Felicia sleep before I reached out to touch her belly. There was no one else I could tell other than the beautiful woman lying in the bed that I was scared of being a dad. Though I was excited, I was scared as shit of messing up. I know what I have to do and the sooner the better.

Felicia started moving around in the bed.

"Your back?" she whispered reaching out to hold my hand.

"Yeah, I'm back. Aunt Sadie will be back tomorrow." I stated. She nodded her head.

"Lay with me." She requested moving over to make room for me. I stood up from the chair and climbed in bed with her. She rested her head on my chest and I held her. *Damn I love this girl.* I thought to myself.

"Do you hurt anywhere?" I asked.

"No, I'm fine right now. Happy you came back though." She spoke into my chest.

"No place better to be than with you." I said into her hair.

"I want you to know I'm handling her ass. I'm already working on it. I swear I been stopped fucking with her crazy ass." I promised.

"I believe you Rah." She reassured me.

"Just trust me and I'll make all this shit go away. You just need to have the baby" I locked my fingers with hers.

Reunited!

Felicia

It's been a few days and I'm still stuck in this damned hospital. Their observation turned into me being dilated a few centimeters. They were saying the baby was almost ready to come and the doctors felt it better to be safe than sorry. I wasn't having any contractions yet and restless was an understatement. I wanted the baby to get here already. Rah visited in the morning and evening so I was left here during the day going crazy by myself.

A few times I spotted him talking to a few of the women at the receptionist area. They were always smiling in his damn face, it was starting to get to me. I prided myself on not being the jealous type but after the fight that landed me here it was starting to rear its ugly head. What could be so important about talking and flirting with the nurses? He left about an hour ago and I was left to watch television. My day was filled with monotony and I wanted to go home to my comfortable bed. Life felt like it was going on around me and I was stuck in a hospital. I buzzed a nurse and asked for a cup of ice chips. She bought it to be and snuck in a red Jell-O cup. That made me feel better for a little bit before I drifted off to sleep. Raheim and I haven't discussed boy names for the baby but I had a feeling that I'd just know the moment I laid eyes on him.

When I woke up the sound of Emeril filled the mid-sized room as he showed us how to make cornbread made with Italian sausage.

"Ms. Orton, the doctor says he'd like for you to try to walk around a little today. I'll have a nurse come and escort you." The redheaded nurse said with a pleasant smile on her face.

"I'll walk her." A familiar voice spoke. I tilted my head to see the person walking into my room. It was my sister Sandy.

"Oh my God!" I sang out. Tears filled my eyes quickly. I haven't seen my sister in almost six years.

"What are you doing here?" I asked as she leaned over for a hug.

"I spoke with your friend Raheim and he told me that you were here." She informed me. I remembered telling him about my sister and my unusual relationship with my mother but he didn't tell me that he spoke with her.

"He's my boyfriend and also the baby's father." I corrected. I was tired of feeling like I needed to apologize "I can't believe this though." I said wiping my eyes. She moved the covers and offered me her arm so I could get up for my walk.

We began walking slowly around the hospital.

"Mommy told me you're trying to go to school to become a lawyer." I started the conversation off.

"Yes, but I'm sure she told you how I'm selling my soul to the devil by trying to leave." She smirked.

"Yeah she did. Says you're acting like me. Now imagine that. If she really knew you were the rebellious one she might really have a heart attack." I joked making my sister laugh.

"I'm sorry for not talking to you all this time. I was just trying to make mama happy but you were right for leaving." She comforted me. Her words made me cry. Being pregnant made me much more emotional.

"How long are you staying?" I asked.

"I don't know. I have a few weeks before I need to start classes so I'm open. Raheim was really generous. He's paying for my hotel stay. Girl he's gorgeous. Do he got any brothers?" she joked.

"His only brother was killed a few weeks ago." I answered with sadness in my tone.

"I'm sorry. I didn't know." She apologized.

"I know, it's alright just don't mention it to him. He's still hurt." I explained.

When I looked up we were making our way back to my room. It felt like we were walking forever. My lower back was aching. As I walked back into my room an unbelievable pain shot across my stomach.

"Oh no, no, no, no, no" I said trying to hold on to the arm of the chair.

"You ok?" Sandy asked.

"No, oh my God it hurts." I groaned. My stomach felt tight and seized with pain.

"I'll be right back." Sandy ran out the room toward the nurse's station.

The pain subsided and I was able to get back into the bed. A young black nurse came into my room. Her hair was pulled into a ponytail.

"Did you just have a contraction?" she asked.

"Yes." I answered.

"Alright keep an eye on the clock and let me know when you feel another one ok? She said cheerfully.

"This is so exciting." Sandy said, standing over me as the nurse checked my vitals and reconnected me to a machine.

"Yeah, real exciting." I responded sarcastically. We talked for another twenty minutes before the pain ripped through me unexpectantly.

"Oh no. Where's Raheim? I need him here!" I screamed through the pain. The intensity of this contraction was much worse than the first.

"I'll call him." Sandy volunteered. "What's him number?" she asked

"It's in my phone, ouch." I yelled. Once the pain subsided I asked her to pass me my cell.

I hit the speed dial number for Raheim and waited for him to pick up. He finally answered after the third ring.

"You better get here quick. I'm about to have the baby. I'm already have contractions." I yelled into the phone.

"Damn, I'm on my way." He said. Though I heard him I felt like crying. This was really happening but I need the baby to wait a few minutes longer. I don't want to have him without Raheim here.

"Is he coming?" My sister asked as I ended the call.

"Yeah he's on his way. I hope he hurries up."

"What was that twenty minutes apart? Hopefully he gets here fast." She tried to calm me. Though I wished my mom would have come I was happy to have my sister here with me. She flipped the television back on and turned to an old episode of America's funniest videos which made me laugh. Things quickly turned upsetting when another wave of painful contractions seized my belly bringing on the urge to push.

"Please God, I don't want to do this without him here." I prayed aloud.

I Know What He Meant

Raheim

There was no business with Dre, I just told Felicia that

to get out of the hospital. I had a few surprises lined up for

her. She didn't mention her sister getting there but I knew

she made it because I dropped her off at the hospital

myself. Her going into labor altered my plans a little but the

mission was still the same. I ran over to pick up my aunt

and we headed over to the hospital.

"You ready?" she asked looking me in the face

"Pretty ready." I said calmly even though I was

nervous as shit.

"You'll be fine." She comforted. My heart was

pounding. All of this was still surreal, a few times today I

reached for my phone to dial Amir and remembered he

wasn't with me. I had to shake the feeling before it made

me emotional. I didn't tell her but I rented us a new spot in

the University City area. It was a bit upscale, a college

town that I knew Felicia would love. Her girls were helping me set the furniture up that I spent the last few days buying. They were decorating and putting feminine touches on for her.

"I need to make a stop." I said pulling up to a floral shop. I really wasn't good with all of the romantic stuff but my aunt told me to grab her a bouquet of red roses. I paid the guy for two dozen and a blue teddy bear. She held the flowers the rest of the way to the hospital. When we got there we let reception know we were visiting Felicia and headed back to her room. My aunt walked in the room, while I stopped at the nurse's station.

"It has to be now." I said and they nodded.

The sight when I walked in was scary, she was clenching the bedrail with sheer pain written across her face. A nurse was there monitoring her contraction. Sandy turned to look at us with a smile on her face.

"You're about to be a daddy." She said. My aunt passed me the bouquet and I took a deep breath and waited for the contraction to subside.

"Here baby." I gave her the flowers. She looked happy and miserable all at once.

"Thank you, I'm so glad you're here." She said with a relieved tone. Before she could get in another word a nurse came into the room carrying a candle and an envelope with the word **'WILL'** written across the front. Felicia looked confused. The nurse sat it on the bed and turned and walked toward the doorway. Another shorter, black nurse came in behind her holding a candle and an envelope with the word **'YOU'** written on it and sat it on the bed and turned to walk away. The next nurse followed suite and approached the bed with another scented candle and an envelope with the word **'MARRY'** written across it. Sandy slowly put her hand up to her mouth and Felicia looked surprised. When the nurse turned to leave I dropped to one knee beside the bed and pulled out a blue Tiffany box from my pants pocket.

"What are you doing?" Felicia asked softly with a smile on her face. I opened the box, displaying the huge two carat diamond engagement ring.

"Felicia, I knew you were special the moment I saw you but what I didn't know then was how perfect for me you actually are. You are the only woman on the planet who makes me feel complete and I want to feel this way forever. I would love to be your husband. Will you marry me?" I asked.

With a big smile and tears running down her face she nodded her head yes and leaned over to kiss me before another contraction hit and she held onto me tight. In the middle of the contraction she yelled out "YES!" making everyone in the room laugh and run to make her feel more comfortable. This contraction was more intense and it caused her to scream out in pain.

The nurse asked if everyone could wait in the waiting area except for me. I was happy for the alone time with her. We were about to be united by blood with the one person to make us one. After the pain passed she turned over to look at me. Sweat was above her eyebrow.

"I can't believe you planned that." She said.

"Couldn't have the mother of my child sitting in the delivery room without a ring on it. I know how much that bothers you babe." There was a lot that she didn't say that I picked up on. Having other women question if she was married always made her cringe. I loved her and couldn't think of anywhere I'd rather be than here and it felt right.

The anesthesiologist was ready to give her an epidural so I watched them wheel her to a different room. They let me know that her contractions were starting to come in a lot closer together and that I would have to get prepped to be in the operating room with her when they were done with the epidural. Shit was about to get real were my only thoughts. For a brief moment I felt closer to my dad. I wondered if he felt this way when I was born. My Aunt Sadie told me that he was at the hospital and so was she the night I came into the world and my dad said it was the best night of his life. I knew what he meant!

It's a Boy!

Felicia

Having a long ass needle pumping numbing medicine into your spine wasn't as bad as I thought it would be. I didn't have much time to think over the excitement of Rah's proposal but I planned on recapping it when the baby arrived. We were already in the delivery room with me floating on cloud nine now that I could no longer feel the contractions. Raheim was standing on the side of me as the doctors were yelling orders for me to push.

I pushed with all of my might and tried not to break Raheim's hand as I did it.

"Final push, you're almost there." The doctor spoke through his face mask. I was tired and wanted to stop going. Raheim was stroking my hair and occasionally wiping sweat from my eyebrows. I gave the last push until the doctor held the baby in his hands by his feet and spanked him on the butt. He was covered in blood and other gunk from my placenta.

"It's a boy." The doctor announced. It wasn't until I heard his tiny cry slice the air that I began to cry like a baby. Raheim kissed me.

"Dad, you can cut the umbilical cord." A nurse said handing Raheim a pair of surgical scissors. He cut it nervously. Seconds later they were resting the baby on my chest close to my face for a moment.

"Oh my God, he's so beautiful." I said. I glanced up at Raheim and he looked amazed at the tiny baby with the head full thick, dark curls. A nurse came to pick up the baby.

"Let's get him all cleaned up." She stated before walking him over to the other side of the room.

"We did that." I said before Raheim leaned down to kiss me again.

"Yeah, we did." He confirmed. My heart felt connected to his in that moment. He gave me two greatest gifts. One is to be the mother of his child and second is to be his wife. I planned on being the best at both.

After the baby was cleaned up they wrapped him in a blue blanket and slipped a tiny cream colored hat to cover his head and placed him back in my arms.

"We're going to take you back over to your room in a few minutes." One of the taller nurses said. It wasn't until I was wheeled back to my room and Raheim was sitting beside me that we got to revel in our little boy.

"We didn't pick out a name." Raheim said looking down at him. He looked so tiny in my arms. I reached my arms out handing him his son. He looked nervous like he thought he might break him.

"His name is Rahmir Carlos Starz. To honor you and your brother and father." My eyes didn't leave his face. He looked at me with more love than I've ever seen him have before. Tears poured over his eyes as he looked down at our son.

"Rahmir, I love it." He confirmed.

"Thank God he has my perfectly shaped head." I joked to lighten the mood.

"Do you think we should call in Aunt Sadie and my sister?" I asked. He kissed Rahmir before placing him back in my arms.

"I'll go get them." He stated before leaning over to kiss me one last time.

"I love you Rah." I said into his mouth.

"I love you more." He answered before walking out toward the waiting room.

How quickly things change in a year. I said to myself.

Singing the Blues

Kelly

For three days I've stayed in bed, using sick days to cover the time off. Raheim planned on killing me that day in my bathroom and it made me sick to think about. *What makes her better than me?* I asked myself a million times a day. He kept calling me crazy but I was tired of having dudes think it was ok to take pussy without claiming me and Raheim is the one I really wanted.

He was the prize, all my girls thought he was hot. I showed my mom pictures of him and she even said if I didn't claim his ass she would. I know I have an attitude problem but how can I not when I gave him an ultimatum and he walks out like I didn't mean shit. Then he has the nerve to get a chick pregnant. All I wanted was to feel special like I meant something to him and granted I shouldn't have hit on a pregnant chick but she had a smart ass mouth.

My cell phone rang, I looked at it before hitting ignore. I didn't feel like talking to Shay. She called again so I answered.

"What?" I asked with my face buried in my covers.

"Get your ass up and get dressed. I'm on my way over. I'm not playing Kelly get the fuck up. How you got this nigga twisting your damn head?" she asked rhetorically.

"You don't understand, I love him." I confessed. She sighed heavily before shouting.

"Bitch, I'm only going to tell you this once. His ass has moved on and so should you. He obviously ain't worth shit so be glad you not the chick having his kid." She gave it to me straight. The words pierced through me. Shay was always good for telling you the truth even if it hurt and hurt it did.

"Open your door, I'm a few blocks away." She said before ending the call. I grudgingly pulled myself from the bed and shuffled to the front door to leave it unlocked.

My apartment looked like a tornado hit it. Clothes were thrown everywhere, Chinese food cartons and empty pizza boxes were sitting on my coffee table and the floor in front of the couch. I didn't have any energy to clean up so I flopped down on the sofa and waited for her to get here. A few minutes later she hit the ringer, I buzzed her in and waited for her to come up the stairs. All of my Essence magazines were tossed everywhere. She walked in without knocking. Her hand immediately went to her nose.

"Are you fucking kidding me? I can't believe you in here acting like this." She said anger lining her voice.

"I didn't ask you to come here." I snapped.

"You didn't have to ask because I'm your girl. C'mon let's clean up. Where is your damn trash bags?" She marched through the living room toward the kitchen and searched each cabinet.

"I know you love him boo but you either let him go or figure out how to get him back. You can't be fucking with his baby mom cause that ain't shit can land your ass in jail." She said while yanking a trash bag from under the kitchen sink.

"Can you just go? You don't fucking understand. He embarrassed me in fucking public Shay. He pushed me on the ground like I wasn't shit. I've been fucking this nigga for two years and that's how he do me. He lucky I don't have no brothers cause I'd have em fuck his ass up for that." I ranted.

"When's the last time you were with him ma?" she asked with irritation on her face like she knew something I didn't know.

"What you mean?" I snapped.

"Look Kel, I know your ass love him an all that shit but I already know you ain't been seeing his ass for a while. Whenever he was coming over you always made sure you called me before he got there to brag. He ain't been coming around for a few months now and you can like to Lakeisha and all them but I know you. You can do better than him though." Her words sliced through me. She was right we've known each other since elementary school. I didn't have Raheim and no matter how much faking I did I couldn't bring him back.

The problem was I couldn't let him go. I've never been with a dude who looked as good as Raheim, who was a boss and something about him rejecting me made me want him even more.

"I just need him to turn on that pregnant bitch long enough to see that he already has the perfect chick for him." I said more to myself but Shay heard it.

"I got your back no matter how you go about shit but I'm telling you now you can't be sitting around acting all whipped and shit cause that ain't attractive." She snapped before tossing old containers into the trash bag.

All about the Baby!

Felicia

I was released from the hospital this morning. The nurse just bought in my discharge papers and gave us a baby bag filled with bottles of formula, diapers and a few blankets. Rah was on his way up with the car seat. I couldn't stop looking at my handsome baby boy with his long, thick eye lashes and father's green eyes. He looked so much like Raheim it was crazy. His skin was a golden brown and his tiny body was still covered in fuzz.

The nurse came around with a wheelchair just as Rah was walking into the room. He was holding the blue and white car seat with rockets and stars.

"Here, I'll take him." Raheim lifted the baby from my arms and placed him into the car seat to strap him for me. I couldn't keep my eyes off him.

"You stand up and sit in the wheelchair and we'll roll you down to the lobby." The nurse spoke in semi-annoying whiny voice. I stood slowly off the bed glad he brought me a pair of yoga pants and a t-shirt.

"Hold up." Rah said, sitting the car seat on the bed and grabbing the vase with my roses.

"Give those balloons to one of the other girls here." He instructed the nurse.

We were off. The nurse wheeled me down with Raheim carrying our son to the lobby. He placed the car seat in my lap as he jogged over to bring the car around.

"You have such a beautiful baby." The nurse looked down on him admiringly.

"Thanks." I stated.

"I hope you and your husband the best." She said squeezing my arm as Raheim pulled up and got out.

Her words hit me and made my eyes water.

"What's the matter?" he asked.

"I'm just happy." I responded and I was. My life was nothing shy of perfect right now and I hoped it stayed like this forever. After strapping the baby in securely he helped me into the passenger seat.

"Where's my sister and Aunt Sadie?" I asked curiously as he pulled off from the hospital parking lot.

"They back at the house waiting for us. You feel ok?" he reached over and squeezed my hand.

"Yes I'm perfect. Can't wait to sleep in our bed though." I confessed.

"Yeah, I miss you being there too. I made everything comfortable for you though and Aunt Sadie made you some of her fish and mashed potatoes." He informed me. I looked over at the man who never ceased to amaze me. I underestimated his love a year ago. He not only proved me wrong but he proved to be more capable of love than he even realizes.

"Your sister is funny as hell though. She asked me to hook her up with one of my boys." He laughed. I was shocked.

"Yeah right, Sandy's ass ain't trying to get caught up."
I laughed.

"You know what's funny babe? I think her and Amir
would have gotten along. They both talk that bible stuff."
He observed. I took a moment to think about it before
laughing.

"You know I think you're right." I looked out the
window and realized he wasn't going near either of our
places.

"Where you going Rah?" I asked. He pulled up in front
of an oversized house in University City. The block was
shaded by tall trees.

"What is this?" I asked as he jumped out of the car.

"You'll see." He said with a sexy smile on his lips. He
walked around to my side of the car and opened the door. I
stepped out deciding to keep quiet. I really didn't feel like
visiting anyone though. He reached in and unstrapped the
baby and held my hand up the small flight of stairs. When

he got to the front door he rang the doorbell and we both waited for someone to open the door. My sister Sandy appeared at the door and gave me a big hug.

"Welcome home sis." She sang happily in my ear.

"Wait what? This isn't my house." I responded.

"It is now." Rah said before stepping to the side for me to walk in. The living room was huge and the walls were covered with some of my favorite art back at my house.

"What's going on Raheim?" I turned around to ask.

"We were both going back and forth from my place to yours and I thought we should start fresh with our own place. Me, you and our baby can start here." He said putting one arm around my waist and pulling me closer to him. I looked up into his gorgeous face and kissed him softly. He kissed me back like he forgot we weren't alone.

"That's how y'all got in trouble in the first place." His aunt said coming from the kitchen. We all laughed as she reached for Rahmir in the car seat.

"Let me see my nephew." She cooed.

"No, he's your grandson." Raheim corrected making her smile.

"Well he's a handsome grandson." She talked to the baby using a baby voice. I knew then that I'd have to visit my mama to introduce her to both my husband to be and son. It wouldn't be difficult but I'm sure once she saw him she'd make it all about the baby.

Not as Hard as it Looks

Raheim

It's been eight weeks since we brought little man home. I hired a cleaning lady to keep the house clean so Felicia didn't have to worry about anything but me and the baby. I was leaning back on the couch with Rahmir laying on my chest sleeping. A game was on and Felicia was upstairs taking a shower.

"Raheim come here for a minute." She yelled down at me. I stood up carefully and walked us both up the stairs into the bedroom. Felicia was lying across the bed completely naked but covered by a sheet.

"Damn, what's going on?" I asked. My dick started to rise. I walked Rahmir over to his bassinet and lay him down on his back. He squirmed for a minute but drifted back to sleep.

The doctor gave us the green light to have sex after the sixth week mark but she wasn't ready. Not that she didn't handle business because she made sure she gave me the best damn head jobs a man could ask for.

"What you up here trying to start?" I asked playfully, laying on top of her.

"I miss you is all." She said coyly. I kissed her on the lips again. Grinding my hardness into her leg. My lips found its way to her collarbone then between her breasts. Her boobs were fuller now and I intended on enjoying them. I squeezed her nipples gently through the sheet before lifting enough to pull it away from her.

My dick was hard enough to punch a hole in a wall, so foreplay wasn't going to be a main attraction today. I've been waiting for this moment for the past eight weeks. I pulled my shirt up and she helped me lift it off. Before I could reach my jeans she leaned up and told me to get on my back. I shifted my body and laid down when she unzipped my jeans and reached inside to squeeze firmly. I moaned quietly. In one smooth motion she pulled my jeans off and climbed on my lap ready to ride. I looked up at her full tits and reached for her nipples as she eased down slowly. I fought the urge to moan loudly. She rode me slowly while leaning down to kiss me softly. It wasn't until she leaned back again that she moved faster. I gripped her waist as she came up and down harder and faster on my hardness. I wanted to prolong the orgasm but she felt so warm and soft inside.

"Yes, damn girl." I looked up at her in amazement as she had a smile playing on her beautiful full lips.

"You like that?" she asked moving in circles and then up and down again.

"Yes, I do." I said barely able to talk.

"Good!" she said before bouncing up and down faster. She brought me close to the edge of an orgasm causing me to grab her ass firmly.

"Shit! Ahhhh, I'm coming." I said, one hand gripping her ass the other grabbing the sheets.

"I miss you too." She laid down on me as I tried to catch my breath.

"Waaaaaaaa, Waaaaaaaa" Rahmir let us know he was awake. We both laughed as I stood up and slipped on my boxers and walked over to his bassinet.

"You can't be waking up little man when your dad's trying to make a move on your mama." I said picking him up. He was still small but his tan skin was becoming more pronounced. His black hair was curlier. He looked like the poster child for baby models.

"Did you feed him?" she asked.

"Yeah about an hour ago." I answered laying back on the bed.

"Check his pamper." She said while squeezing his diaper.

"That's it, you need your daddy to change your diaper huh? Tell daddy." She cooed into his face. He smiled at the sound of her voice.

"Where is his diapers?" I asked standing up to grab them.

"Over there." She answered pointing toward the dresser. I grabbed the bag and his baby wipes.

"Here you go." I put them in front of her.

"Do you see this Mir? Your dad trying to pass you off to me. Well the next poopy diaper going straight over to him." She looked me direct in the eye when she said it, making me laugh.

"No, I got his one." I unfastened his diaper and removed the wet one, using the wipes to clean his area before putting him on a dry diaper. Both Felicia and my aunt showed me how to do it until I felt like a pro.

For a moment I was worried about not being a good dad but then I realized it wasn't as hard as others would lead you to believe. I had good genes and good taste. Rahmir couldn't have come at a more perfect time. A few nights ago the news made mention of the chick I blasted.

Saying she was a missing person. I couldn't help but think she wasn't missing she was cut up in a few dozen pieces and apart of the house Dre called his trap spot. I laid low happily spending time with Felicia and the baby only leaving the house to take her out to lunch or dinner and doctor's appointments.

"What now sexy mama." I said placing Rahmir on my chest and pulling her into me as we both lay on or backs.

"I could eat. You need to get your energy up anyway we going again later on tonight." She whispered into my mouth. My dick got hard again at the promise of much missed sex later.

"Oh, we'll be ready." I mentioned both me and my lower half. She pecked my lips.

"Good. Now go get dressed so we can head out." She demanded while picking the baby up from my chest.

"How about this, you get real sexy, I'll call my mom and have her watch the baby while I treat my woman to a nice dinner." I suggested. It's been awhile since either of us dressed up to go on a real date.

Felicia's face lit up which made me feel good.

"Ok." She answered walking quickly over to her closet. I dialed Aunt Sadie's number.

"Hello?' she answered.

"Hey. I have a question for you. I want to take Felicia out to dinner. Do you mind watching little man?" I asked already sure of her answer.

"Are you kidding me? Bring me my baby." She sang into the phone. He was already spoiled.

"Alright. We'll be there." I informed her.

"Pack him an overnight bag. You two enjoy your night and we'll be ok until tomorrow." She offered. I agreed before hitting the end button.

"She says he can stay the night." I said aloud. Felicia turned, still naked with a smile on her face.

"Thanks babe." She mouthed. She used one hand to cover her stomach which was still a little fluffy from the pregnancy. I walked over to her and wrapped my arms around her from behind.

"Why are you trying to cover up?" I asked softy into her hair.

"I don't know." She answered shyly.

"Because you know I think you're gorgeous. I love every inch of you and the fact that you gave birth to our son makes you sexier." She turned to face me and stood on her tip-toes to give me a long, deep kiss.

We both took another shower before Felicia slipped on a sexy red dress that accentuated all of her curves. It also made her new larger cleavage stand out more. I wasn't sure how I would manage getting through the night. Rahmir drifted in and out of sleep as Felicia fixed her hair and makeup, not that she needed to. I put on a pair of my fitted

Armani dress pants and a white dress shirt with a red and white pinstriped tie.

My uncle showed me how to dress. He always told me and Amir that important men wore suits. I remembered that and preferred dressing nice over dressing street any day of the week.

When she was all done we wrapped the baby and put him in his car seat. She grabbed his baby bag as I carried him out to the car. I strapped him in and got in the driver side after opening and closing the door for her. The air was a fresh, not too hot but not too cold. I put on a few old school jams as we headed over to my Aunt's house. Felicia reached over and stroked the back of my neck. *This is the life, this is all I've been looking for.* I said to myself. It's incredible how important Felicia makes me feel. I've never felt cared for, missed or needed like she's managed to make me feel.

My aunt was already standing by the door waiting for us to get there. I could barely park before she was opening the back door to grab Rahmir from his car seat.

"Raheim bring in his car seat. Felicia you look beautiful, is that a new lipstick color?" She asked all in one breathe.

"Yeah, I got it a week ago. Thanks so much for watching him." Felicia said stepping out of the car to give the baby a kiss.

"He'll be fine, you two go have fun and don't be trying to make no more babies. It's too early for all that." She joked, looking at me. I laughed with my hands in the air.

"I ain't promising you nothing." I responded making us all laugh. It took us another five minutes to say goodbye with Felicia continuously kissing Rahmir.

"Come on babe." I insisted.

"Alright, alright. It's just the first time we're leaving him over night." She confessed.

"He'll be ok." I promised.

"So where you taking me?" she asked while putting on her seatbelt.

"I was thinking we could eat at that restaurant in back of the art museum." I said glancing her way briefly.

"Awww, Rah. I've always wanted to go there." She said with excitement. You treat me so good." She said leaning over to kiss me on the cheek.

"You gone mark me up with your lipstick." I joked. "No I'm not this is that good stuff, color stay. See." She reached over and wiped my face with two fingers to prove her point.

I couldn't believe that I was sitting across from the woman I wanted to marry. *Damn life changes so fast.* I thought.

Beautiful Days turn into Beautiful Nights
Felicia

What I love about Raheim is how much effort he has put into making me happy. I haven't had to complain about him ripping and running in the streets after the baby came home. I think he genuinely loves having his own family. It was hard leaving the baby with his aunt overnight but I really think we needed our alone time. He made me feel beautiful, which makes me love him even more. We drove up to the museum and walked holding hands up the stairs. There were other nicely dressed couples going in the same direction. It was a beautiful day for romance. I searched the faces of everyone there but none looked as happy as I felt right now.

As we waited for the waitress to escort us to a table I turned into Raheim as he wrapped his arms around me and I rested my head on his shoulder.

"You cold?" he asked.

"No, your arms are keeping me warm." I said. Rah, loved being needed, it made him feel important so I made it my job to let him know me and the baby need him every day. The waitress in her tight black dress told us to follow her. We got an outdoor table close to the view of the water. I couldn't help smiling. The ambiance was romantic.

"Let me find out you're secretly romantic." I said with a smile.

"So you still think it's a secret huh?" he smirked.

"I guess not. Seriously though Rah, I really needed this tonight." I thanked him.

"I know, that's why I suggested it. So when you plan on talking about the wedding?" He asked, looking me dead in the eye.

Of course I was excited to marry him but I'm not stupid. What attracted him to me in the first place was my slow to act personality. I'm not in a rush to get down the aisle but I knew I couldn't take forever.

"Wasn't sure what time frame would work best for you." I put it back on him.

"I'm ready to do it tomorrow but you can pick the date and I'll give you a budget. You can have anything you want though. Money ain't a problem." He said. I've been dreaming about my wedding since I was five. But it is funny how having the right man makes none of that seem important.

"Can we get married in Jamaica?" I asked.

"We can get married on the moon if you want to. I'm serious Felicia. I never been this happy with anybody so whatever you want it's yours." He smiled, his gorgeous smile making me wet.

After ordering our drinks I excused myself to go the bathroom. Tonight was all about being grown and sexy and after having Rahmir I haven't been feeling too beautiful or sexy for that matter. I used the bathroom and slipped my lace thongs off, folding them in my hands. I quickly washed my hands and checked my makeup before making my way back to the table. When I got there I stopped beside Rah and slipped my panties into his hand. He looked quickly and smiled before sliding them into his pocket.

"Shit girl. " He said with an 'I want to fuck you right here' face. I blew him a kiss, fully aware that our beautiful day was going to end in a very beautiful night.

Free At Last

Janet

My information panned out and they were able to find freezers filled with human remains in Jimmy's mechanic shop. He had an additional room built to store all of the freezers. His sadistic ass enjoyed having them there like sick trophies. Not to mention the large amounts of coke he had stored I was called down to the administrator's office.

"Ms. Starz, it looks like you're due to be released tomorrow." She stated with an arrogant stare.

"Yes, I know thanks." I said. Nothing this bitch or anyone else could say to bring me down. After years of being in this living nightmare I would finally be free to walk in the world. My mom and aunt said they would be here tomorrow morning to pick me up. I just had to stay low key for one more day. When bitches find out you're getting out they have a tendency to start shit.

I was only cool with one person and that was Wanda my roommate. I already let her know she could have all of my stuff. I didn't want to take anything with me other than the pictures of my kids and the letters Amir and my mom wrote me. After being given discharge instructions I was sent back to my room. I fought the feeling of anxiousness that threatened to make me jump up and down with happiness.

When I got back to my cell she was there sitting on her bed reading. She lowered her book when I walked in.

"So it's official huh?" she said sadly.

"Yeah, I'm outta here tomorrow morning." I said refraining from sounding too happy.

"What's the first thing you're gonna do?" she asked wishfully.

"I'm going straight to McDonald's and getting a burger and a big ass milk shake. Then I'm going to get my hair done and buy a fly outfit. I swear if I never see khaki again in my life it will still be too soon." I stated while flopping down on my cot.

"I know that's right." She added. I already went through my stuff the day before and realized that the last fifteen years of my life boiled down to a box full of letters, books I've read and various items left from commissary.

I spent the rest of my day watching television in the rec room. I didn't care what was on. I just needed a distraction to keep my mind off of my freedom. I kept it hush-hush so I didn't provoke jealousy or raise suspicion. It felt like forever before we had to go back to our cells for final count. After that it was lights out. I happily laid down on my bunk ready to close my eyes. However, Wanda had different plans. She slid down on to my bed.

"You up for a little going away head?" she asked in a whispered tone.

"Sure why not." I responded. As soon as she heard my answer she was reaching under my shirt to squeeze my tits.

Wanda was great at what she did but I had to be quiet. She raised my shirt and pulled my bra down aggressively. I closed my eyes and pictured Carlos. Her warm mouth found their way to my nipple and she began kissing and sucking. I reaching for her hand and slid it down between my legs. She followed suit and reached in between my legs. I spread them for her while she pulled them down. The thought of freedom made me hornier.

"Eat me." I demanded softly. She obeyed and slid her body to the floor between my legs where she yanked my pants down to my ankles. My breath caught in my throat as her mouth met my clit.

After making me cum harder than any other time before she laid beside me for a moment.

"Don't forget to write." She whispered. I promised both knowing it was a lie. She's been my roommate for the last ten years so we felt like sisters but the truth is we were only held together by bars.

The morning couldn't come fast enough. I woke up and realized this was the last day I'd be counted. It would be the last time I went to eat breakfast in the cafeteria. I couldn't wait to get going. I ate half of my food and slid the rest to Wanda. She was happy to get it. I went back to my room and waited until my name was called. Wanda met me there and gave me a big hug when they called me over the loud speaker. I walked proudly holding my box of books and letters to the processing center. All eyes were on me. Some were filled with envy but I didn't give a damn. Correctional officer Morris gave me a bag with the clothes I was wearing when they arrested me. I almost forgot the dress. It was a black knee length tank top dress with pockets on both sides and a pair of flip flops. I took the plastic bag and looked it over. A small wad of cash was there along with a pair of diamond hooped earrings. I fought the urge to smile.

"Get changed here" She said while watching me dress. I slipped my ugly khaki prison uniform over my head and excitedly put on the dress. The cotton material felt so soft. It was the first time I've worn a dress in over fifteen years. I took off the shoes and slipped on the flip flops. My feet even felt free. After changing I was taken to the front desk where I needed to sign out. The pen shook in my hand as I signed my name on the dotted line.

C.O Morris escorted me to the front door and then through the gates where I spotted a car parked out front. Moments later my mom stepped out of the passenger side.

"I wish you the best Ms. Starz and I hope I never see you here again." She said giving me her hand to shake. I turned to face her and looked her directly in the eye and said

"I'll die before I come back." We both cracked a smile and I ran toward my mother almost not believing it was happening until I ran through the gates.

"Oh my God!" My mom pulled me into her while my aunt grabbed my box. She started to cry into my shoulder.

"I can't believe you are here. I never thought I'd see this day." She cried. A lump formed in my throat and tears spilled over and down my cheeks.

"I'm here now mama. It'll be ok." I comforted her. My aunt sat my box in her trunk before my mom finally released me. I hugged my aunt before getting into the car and heading toward my mother's house.

"What do you want to do first?" My mom asked.

"I'd really like to stop at McDonald's I'm dying for a big mac and a milkshake." I said like a child waking up on Christmas morning.

"McDonald's it is." My aunt said. I rolled down my window and sucked in the fresh air. It's amazing how good free air smells. I looked at the houses, the cars which looked way different from what I remembered. It was in that moment that the weight of my freedom came crashing down on me. A heaviness lifted from my chest and I began to cry. I hated that Amir wasn't here to see this. That he wasn't there to meet me. My aunt and mother both sat quiet as I cried like a baby. For the first time in fifteen years it felt safe to show emotion. All of the feelings I kept bottled up inside flowed out of me like a river. I would allow myself to cry this time but from here on out I was going to be a better me, the best version of myself. But I really couldn't wait to get dolled up, to feel like a woman.

"I got a room all ready for you at the house. I'm just so glad you're home Janet. We're going to have a bar-b-que in your honor on Saturday." She continued her rant. It felt good to hear her talking with no limitations on what to talk about.

"I would like that mama. Where's dad?" I asked wiping my face. They both got quiet.

After I shot Carlos things between my father and I were very strained and he told me I was disowned by him. He couldn't be happy about me coming home.

"Janet, your father will come around. It's just gonna take some time." She started.

"I get it, you don't need to sugarcoat it for me ma. I'm just happy to be home. I'll try to find work and get my own place soon enough ok." I reached up and squeezed her shoulder.

My aunt pulled into the McDonald's drive thru for me to place an order. When she pulled around to pay my mother reached for her purse.

"No mom I got it." I pulled the small wad of cash from my dress pocket and handed the lady a ten dollar bill. She gave me my change and we pulled up to the second window where I collected my food. I grabbed the bag hungrily and damn near ripped the bag apart. The moment my teeth sank into the burger I fell back into the backseat and sighed.

"Taste good huh?" My mom asked smiling.

"Like you wouldn't believe." I said between chewing. The closer we got to my old neighborhood the more I felt like getting my hair done.

"Ma, do you think it would be ok if we stop at a salon. I've been dying to get my hair curled.

"It's ok with me if it's ok with your aunt." She responded.

"Of course it is." My aunt Bunnie smiled at me.

Everything was so different and looked so much smaller than I remembered. My aunt parked in front of a walk-in's welcomed salon that was empty.

"I want my hair pressed." I said to a beautiful Jamaican woman wearing a burgundy colored apron.

"Ok, so a Brazilian blow out?" She stated. I was lost.

"I don't know what that is." I stated ignorantly. She handed me a photo album and flipped the pages til she reached what she was referring to.

"Yes exactly." I answered. My natural hair was in the middle of my back. I've grown it for the last fifteen years and kept it braided.

We were done in two hours and I walked out of the salon feeling like a million bucks. My mother oohed and aahed over my hair. It flowed like silk and moved in the wind. My aunt drove me to Springfield mall where I was able to pick out a few fly outfits. I had a flashback of getting dressed up for Carlos. I shook the thought, today was about me. I walked out of one of the stores wearing a pair of skinny jeans, a sexy black lace tank top shirt and a pair of black stilettos. I felt like a million dollars. We even stopped at a M.A.C makeup counter where the makeup artist gave me a makeover.

For the remainder of the ride home I wore a big smile on my face. I was back and better than ever. Today I would revel in my newness but tomorrow I would make my way around the streets to see what was good. My aunt apologized that she had to leave once we pulled up to my parent's house. My heart started to pound the closer I got to the door. This would be the first time I've seen my father since I was incarcerated.

"Pops where are you?" I yelled out. He came from out of the kitchen and stopped in his tracks. We were both silent, just staring at one another. He looked much older than I remembered. I studied his face for a long moment.

After examining me from head to toe he turned to walk away. I felt devastated.

"Dad, why are you walking away from me?" I yelled after him. He was going to need to give me an explanation. I walked behind him.

"Pops, talk to me." I begged.

"Janet, there is absolutely nothing I have to say to you. You are already dead to me." He said sharply.

"I'm not dead, I'm right here daddy. Why can't you see that? I'm right here." I raised my voice. My mother stood looking lost in the living room as usual.

"You're not my Janet, you are a loose cannon that doesn't need to be in my house. You're capable of anything and I don't want your ass here." He snapped before walking away for the second time.

The words punched me in my chest making it hard to breathe. I turned to face the front door.

"I need some air." I said while walking back out of the house. My mother was crying after me.
"Janet, don't leave. Please stay." She begged with tears streaming down her face.

"I'll be back. I need some air." I said without turning around. I could pretend I didn't care about what my father said but I'd be a liar. For the first time in over fifteen years

I feel completely lost. I started walking toward the main avenue looking for a cab. I didn't realize how much I wanted to be held by my father. I needed him to hold me and tell me he still loves me. But he didn't give a damn so I wouldn't either.

It was a long time before a cab came to a stop and allowed me to get in.

"Hello pretty woman where to?" the African cabbie asked. I reached into my pants pocket and pulled out one envelope Amir sent me and gave the cab driver the address. Rage was building beneath my chest. I was supposed to be his daughter. What happened to unconditional love? I ranted internally. I didn't recognize anything around me anymore. The streets no longer looked familiar. It was all one big blur as he drove toward the address I gave him. I gave the cabbie two twenty dollar bills and stepped out of the cab when he pulled me up to the address. Without as much as a second thought I walked confidently up to the front door. There was a small moment of hesitation as I rang the doorbell. Fifty things were running through my head as I waited for the door to be opened. Seconds later my wait was over as the front door swung open. Sadie's familiar face stared back at me with surprise with the faint sound of a baby crying in the distance.

CPSIA information can be obtained at www.ICGtesting.com
Printed in the USA
LVOW10s1603170516

488656LV00002B/399/P